Praise for Ray Keating
and his Pastor Stephen Grant Thrillers...

Warrior Monk: A Pastor Stephen Grant Novel ranked as a Top 10 book on a WORLD magazine June 2013 list.

The host of KFUO radio's "BookTalk" said: "Ray Keating is a great novelist."

Amazon.com readers compare Ray Keating's thrillers to the works of Clancy, Ludlum, Grisham, Cussler, and Morrell.

CNBC's Larry Kudlow called *Warrior Monk* "a compelling thriller."

Best-selling novelist Paul L. Maier called *Root of All Evil? A Pastor Stephen Grant Novel* "an extraordinarily good read," adding, "Only Ray Keating could come up with a character like Pastor Stephen Grant."

Regarding *An Advent for Religious Liberty: A Pastor Stephen Grant Novel*, "BookTalk" host Rod Zwonitzer declared: "It is exciting reading, and tough to put down... good mystery writing."

U.S. Congressman Peter K᠆ ᠆ ᠆aid *Warrior Monk* is "a fast-moving, riveting read   and tomorrow's – headlines."

From a *LutheranForum.org* review of *Warrior Monk*: "This is a good read, both as pure thriller entertainment and for pondering the Christian mind and milieu in the early twenty first century."

On *An Advent for Religious Liberty*, an Amazom.com reviewer observed: "Keating once again shows he weaves a good story that keeps your interest as well as exploring important topics. Can't wait for the next Stephen Grant novel to come out."

A reviewer from *First Things* website called *Warrior Monk* "a fun adventure romp."

And more comments across the Internet...

"Different and refreshing..."

"It is a pleasure to recommend a book to my friends that promotes Christian virtues, is not stuffy, and is an exciting adventure."

"Highly recommend this book to anyone interested in spies, politics, modern faith and its application to daily life or just interested in a different kind of mystery story."

"This book kept me wanting more..."

"... a book of intrigue."

"A great story. Well written. A real page turner."

"Ray Keating has created a unique and memorable character in Pr. Stephen Grant."

The River

A Pastor Stephen Grant Novel

Ray Keating

This book is a work of fiction. Names, characters, places, events and incidents either are the product of the author's imagination or are used fictitiously. Any resemblance to actual persons, living or dead, events or locales is entirely coincidental.

For more information:
Keating Reports, LLC
P.O. Box 596
Manorville, NY 11949
keatingreports@aol.com

ISBN-10: 1499514174
ISBN-13: 978-1499514179

For my family –
Jonathan,
David
and
Beth

Previous Books by Ray Keating

An Advent for Religious Liberty:
A Pastor Stephen Grant Novel (2012)

Root of All Evil? A Pastor Stephen Grant Novel (2012)

Warrior Monk: A Pastor Stephen Grant Novel (2010)

Discussion Guide for Warrior Monk:
A Pastor Stephen Grant Novel (2011)

In the nonfiction arena...

Unleashing Small Business Through IP:
Protecting Intellectual Property, Driving Entrepreneurship
(2013)

"Chuck" vs. the Business World: Business Tips on TV
(2011)

U.S. by the Numbers:
What's Left, Right, and Wrong with America State by State
(2000)

New York by the Numbers:
State and City in Perpetual Crisis (1997)

D.C. by the Numbers: A State of Failure (1995)

"I will make a way in the wilderness and rivers in the desert."

- Isaiah 43:19

"I have laid waste his hill country and left his heritage to jackals of the desert."

- Malachi 1:3

"On the last day of the feast, the great day, Jesus stood up and cried out, 'If anyone thirsts, let him come to me to drink. Whoever believes in me, as the Scripture has said, "Out of his heart will flow rivers of living water."'"

- John 7:37-38

Prologue

The temperature hit 109°F, but with little humidity. *Dry heat, my ass. It's just damn hot. Period.*

Excessive heat, or cold for that matter, never really bothered Stephen Grant. Thanks to his training as a Navy SEAL and then with the CIA, Grant learned that complaining, especially about the uncontrollable, was a waste of time and energy.

Still, he looked down at the sweat visible through his brown cotton shirt, and then his eyes moved to his partner, Paige Caldwell, sitting across the small table. It either bothered or fascinated him – he couldn't decide – that she looked comfortable, even cool. It was as if she were enjoying an iced drink under an umbrella near the ocean in San Diego, rather than sipping a warm beer in a dusty, outdoor bar in Diyabakir, Turkey, in early July.

"Why aren't you sweating – at all?" asked Grant.

Caldwell smiled seductively. "I did enough of that last night. Didn't you?"

Grant nodded. His mind was not convinced that mixing work and sex was smart, or the right thing to do. But given all that Caldwell and Grant had been through over the last two years – never doubting that each other's back was covered – their intimacies just developed naturally.

Grant and Caldwell seemed to fit together in many ways. Each was self-assured, smart, loyal, willing to take risks, strong, calm amidst danger, and attractive to the opposite sex.

Stephen Grant had an athletic, six-foot build, with green eyes, tanned skin, and short, black hair. Rather typical cargo pants and white sneakers accompanied his brown shirt.

Meanwhile, Paige Caldwell's fit, five-foot-nine-inch body was covered in freckles, accentuated by full, pink lips, a rounded nose, and steely blue eyes now hidden behind sunglasses. Her long, jet-black hair was pulled atop her head with just a few strands hanging down, brushing against her neck and flirting with the shoulders of a white cotton shirt. The shirt hung loosely over a white tank top and tan shorts.

But a difference did exist.

While dedicated to his work, Grant understood that there was more to life than the CIA. He was unable, however, to detect such recognition in Caldwell. She actually loved being consumed by the job. Other than sex, everything Caldwell did somehow tied in to her work with the CIA. Grant often wondered if Paige even saw their encounters in bed as a way for her to find a necessary release that would make her a better operative.

She regularly made fun of Grant for his "outside interests," as Caldwell put it, including his love of history, movies and golf. Stephen also had been an archer since his teenage years, but even Paige had to acknowledge that those skills had come in handy during his earliest time with the agency.

In the end, their relationship was convenient and uncomplicated, which appealed to both of them, at least at this point in their lives.

Grant's official title with the agency was "analyst." He even had a cubicle at Langley. But he was more often than not missing from his desk. He had a unique skill set, which meant often being in the field doing things unknown to those in adjacent cubicles. Caldwell's abilities complemented his well.

Grant and Caldwell were posing as tourists. And as tourists, they'd have to be moving on soon if nothing happened. They'd been sitting at the bar for nearly two hours waiting for a shipment to arrive at a small, dull, stone building just up the street, looking to see who would be receiving and stashing the shipment.

After several weeks of what amounted to detective work, the two operatives hoped that they were about to close this investigation. It was a case they wanted no part of in the first place.

Langley suspected that one of their own on the ground in Turkey – Eric Clark – was running a side business. If their suspicions turned out to be correct, that off-the-books venture would cause quite an international incident if exposed.

Grant and Caldwell were tasked with proving or disproving the agency's fears. If Clark was clean, they were to leave the country without him knowing they had been there. If he was dirty, his mess had to be cleaned up and Clark brought home to deal with the consequences.

With the help of the third member of their team, Edward "Tank" Hoard, Grant and Caldwell found this address to be central to the activity that caught the attention of the agency.

Hoard earned the nickname "Tank" due to his body-builder physique. He manned the team's base of operation in Ankara.

The Turks involved in the smuggling operation had been identified. Hoard assured Grant and Caldwell that they would be arriving with a shipment this afternoon. So, they waited to see if Eric Clark would be showing up as well.

As Grant, Caldwell and Hoard had discovered, this was a careful operation. The thefts were calculated to limit the chances of being caught, while maximizing possible payoffs. There was a certain mathematical precision to the risk-reward tradeoff, and Eric Clark had earned a graduate degree in mathematics before joining the agency.

After taking a sip of beer, Grant whispered, "I'm going to find a bathroom."

Caldwell replied, "No, I don't think so." She nodded her head toward the building under surveillance.

A short, stocky man dressed in jeans and a light gray bush shirt approached. His facial features, except for a bulbous nose, were largely hidden behind sunglasses and a tan bucket hat.

"Crap. That's Clark." Grant was disappointed. He had hoped, despite the mounting evidence, that Clark was clean.

Clark entered the building. Less than five minutes later, a white van pulled up.

Two men got out of the front cab, walked around the vehicle, and opened the back doors. A third man handed wood crates out to each.

"Those are our Turkish accomplices," Caldwell said in a low voice.

Grant grunted his agreement.

After six crates were moved inside, a much larger wood box, roughly six feet long, three feet wide and two feet high, was maneuvered out of the van and into the building by the three men.

"Time to move," declared Grant. He left enough lira on the table to more than cover their tab. They moved into the narrow stone street, and toward the building that Clark and his friends had entered. The untrained eye would see a couple strolling hand in hand. But as they nonchalantly strolled along, their eyes were scanning the road, windows, rooftops and doorways to make sure no one else warranted their attention and concern.

Grant generally disliked being on the ground in an urban setting. It meant that potential enemies could have the high ground, and he'd be a sitting duck. While not expected here, he never ruled anything out during an operation.

Behind them, at the corner of a busier thoroughfare, a street vendor was selling fish from the Tigris. Even though they rested on ice, Grant had serious doubts about fish sold from a cart in this heat.

At the other end of the street, three teenagers kicked around a soccer ball.

Grant found nothing in the streetscape to earn additional worry. He nodded at Caldwell, and they moved smoothly to the blue painted door set against the light, tan stone of the building.

As Paige grabbed the door, and quietly clicked it open, they both drew the Glock 19s that were resting against their backs, hidden under shirts.

Grant moved in first, with the handgun in front of him. He scanned the small room. It was sparsely furnished – two dark wood benches, a long, matching table, and a chair in a corner. No one was in the room. But there was movement through an open doorway heading to the back of the building.

Once again, Grant led the way, with Caldwell close behind.

The four men had opened the long crate, and were looking inside. The three Turks, with their backs turned, had no idea that the stealthy Grant and Caldwell were behind them.

But Eric Clark looked up. His smile melted away into a sad resignation.

Clark said, "Hmmm, apparently, I miscalculated. Langley, I presume."

Caldwell replied, "Sure as hell isn't Dr. Livingstone."

The trio of Turks spun to see who was speaking. Grant and Caldwell's guns earned attention. Unfortunately, the Turks' reactions were to go for their own weapons.

As chaos broke, Clark yelled, "No!" His partners paid no attention.

A short, fat man with little hair but a bushy, dark mustache was the first to move. As he pulled a gun from a shoulder holster, Grant fired off two shots. They both hit the man's chest, quickly spreading blood down his ill-fitting white shirt.

The second man moving into action – medium build, thick black hair and a thin beard – managed to get off a shot in the direction of Grant and Caldwell. But before a second could be fired, Caldwell's 9mm round found its way into the front of the Turkish man's brain.

It was the third person working with Clark who presented the most significant threat. When Grant fired his initial shot, the middle-aged man, with graying hair, pointed nose and thick eyebrows, dove behind three of the stacked crates, pulling a mini-UZI from a canvas bag on the floor. He clicked the 32-round magazine in place, popped up from behind the crates, and fired at the two CIA invaders.

Amidst the hail of bullets, Grant gained cover alongside a heavy cabinet. Caldwell tried to move back through the doorway, but a round found her right calf. She returned fire blindly while falling to the floor.

The middle-aged Turk dropped back down until there was a pause from Caldwell's gun. He popped back up, smiled broadly seeing Paige struggling to move in the direction of the doorway, and repositioned the mini-UZI to get a steadier death shot.

But the Turk's own death came quickly and surprisingly from two directions. Moving in from behind, Eric Clark grabbed the Turk's head with his left arm, while driving a tactical knife into the man's back. At the same time, Grant slid from behind the cabinet across the floor, landing a round in the Turk's stomach.

Clark let the man's body, along with the knife, drop to the floor, and then, staring at the two guns pointed at him, put his hands up.

Without moving his eyes from Clark, Grant said, "Paige, you okay?"

"As they say in those movies you love, it's just a flesh wound. I'll be fine."

"You owe me, again," he replied.

Clark interrupted, "Hey, I helped."

Grant moved toward Clark, with his gun still trained.

As she assessed her wound, Caldwell lectured Clark. "Oh, right, you're such a great asset to the team. You jackass. You're not only a damn thief, but you're, in effect, a traitor. If it came to light that a CIA employee was running a ring smuggling antiquities out of Iraq, it would fuel conspiracy theories across the region."

"Still, I wouldn't allow these men to kill a fellow agency employee. That's got to count in the equation, right?"

Caldwell replied, "What do you want, a fucking gold star?"

Clark ignored her comment, adding, "Besides, who said I was the one running things?"

Grant asked, "What does that mean?"

Clark smiled. "Now, why would I tell you that? I need something to bargain with, to limit my potential losses, don't I?"

Grant looked into the box the four thieves had opened.

Staring up was a bronze figure almost five feet long.

Caldwell limped over and glanced into the crate as well. "Who's that supposed to be?"

Grant responded, "I can't be sure." He looked up and down the figure, noting the carvings of torches and the flames at the bottom. "But if I recall from readings I did after one of my ancient history courses at Valpo, this could be a representation of Girra, a Mesopotamian god of fire. He was worshiped for the role that fire played in purification and in making things like bricks, but also feared for his destructive acts, like setting fields ablaze."

Caldwell rolled her eyes. "Too much information."

Grant smiled at Paige, and then looked at Clark, who still had his hands in the air. Grant tilted his head toward Girra. "That belongs in a museum."

Clark looked bewildered, and shrugged his shoulders. "Ah, okay?"

Grant shook his head. "How do you not know that line?"

Caldwell said, "Okay, I'll say it: 'So do you.' Now that you've gotten another Indiana Jones moment out of the way – God, how many has that been since we were given this job? – could you get Tank on the satphone and let him know what we have?"

Chapter 1

Nearly two decades later

Even with the tremendous growth and legitimization of Las Vegas over the past half-century, it still didn't take very long to drive from the Strip into the desert to dump a body.

Nicky "Two Gloves" Geraci knew of a few convenient spots off Interstate 15 south of the city to make that kind of deposit.

Unfortunately, the body in the trunk was not part of the plan.

Ollie Rice had worked at Casino Beach as a blackjack dealer for just over three years. But hotel management discovered that his well-known interest in very young female guests recently turned violent. That most certainly was not good for business; nor would allowing the story to go public.

Geraci was told to teach Rice a few lessons, then make clear that he would be given one chance to leave Las Vegas.

Unbeknownst to Nicky, or his assistant who was helping dole out the ordered lessons, this blackjack dealer had a heart defect. In fact, even Ollie had no idea there was a ticking time bomb in his chest. A blow from the fist clothed in one of Geraci's two black rubber-composite gloves sent Rice out of his chair.

Even at 62 years old, Geraci was an impressive physical specimen – six feet three inches, muscular, dark eyes, thick silver hair and a matching mustache. When not behind closed doors, custom-made gloves always covered his massive hands. That had been the case since they were badly burned more than thirty years ago when a goon got creative trying to end Geraci's life. The highly corrosive acid did irreparable harm to Nicky's hands. Subsequent plastic surgery could only accomplish so much. But it turned out worse for the goon. It wasn't long before Nicky was tagged with the moniker "Two Gloves," and he wound up embracing it. Two Gloves now had dozens of custom-made gloves, fitting a wide array of occasions and clothing options.

Now, despite the padded carpet, when Ollie hit the floor under Geraci's gloved punch, the time bomb went off.

When Ollie's prone body failed to show any movement, Geraci's assistant checked for a pulse. "No, he's dead, boss."

"Come on. I didn't hit the little shit hard enough."

The two men were silent for several seconds.

The assistant asked, "What do you want to do?"

Geraci glanced at his watch. It was just after 3:30 in the morning. "We're going to move the body to the trunk of the car, and make it disappear."

This conference with Ollie had not taken place in Geraci's usual, luxurious office perched many floors above the Las Vegas Strip. Rather, it was a small, nondescript, one floor office building, with a small parking lot, a couple of turns off North Las Vegas Blvd. A six-foot wall around the front and sides of the parking lot kept most things hidden from casual eyes. The building was used for activities not meant to be stumbled upon at the casinos. It proved handy, though was used less and less frequently as time passed.

No one saw Ollie take his place in the car's spacious trunk, nor later when Geraci and his assistant unceremoniously dumped him in the desert while it was still dark. Before long, the late August sun was rising, and began to drive the thermometer higher. After the 100°F mark was left in the dust, Ollie Rice's pale, pudgy body began to transform. By the time the sun moved lower in the western sky later in the day, the dead dealer's skin had darkened, starting to morph. Another day or two of such intense sun and heat, and it would become a leathery shrink-wrap on his skeleton. After the sun disappeared, though, this mummification process ceased as coyotes pounced. The scavengers tore up skin, feasted on internal organs, pulled apart and dragged away bones.

In a couple of days, only a trained eye could have detected that a body had been there. After a week, no one could have suspected. No one did.

Ollie Rice's body already had been disassembled when a friend alerted the police as to his absence. Rice's father, Gil, was notified, and immediately flew in from Chicago.

Gil Rice never returned to his small home in the Windy City.

Chapter 2

The cool water descended like a gentle waterfall.

When the liquid touched her forehead, Sarah Larson startled. As the water spread into and flowed through her light hair, she apparently grew more irritated.

But if any doubt lingered, Sarah made her discomfort quite clear with the subsequent two streams.

As he scooped the water out of the baptismal font in the sanctuary of St. Mary's Lutheran Church and deposited it on Sarah's tiny head, Pastor Zackary Charmichael announced, "I baptize you in the name of the Father ... and in the name of the Son ... and in the name of the Holy Spirit."

Sarah cried loudly, grabbed the microphone clipped on Pastor Charmichael's chasuble, and tugged. She showed real strength for a four-month old.

The loud, swishing sounds emanating from speakers around the room generated laughs among the 240 or so parishioners and guests. Sarah's parents, Pam and Scott Larson, smiled, each with moist eyes. The godparents – Pam's sister Lisa and St. Mary's own Pastor Stephen Grant – joined in the laughter, each beaming at their godchild.

Pastor Grant thought, *Welcome, beautiful baby Sarah, into life in Christ.*

Stephen could not resist a quick glance over his shoulder at the woman sitting in the second pew on the pulpit side. His wife was staring back. Her smile captivated him, as always. With her fair skin, sharp facial features – though with a slightly upturned nose – and short, dark auburn hair, she radiated a unique, warm beauty.

Stephen often found himself thanking God for Jennifer, and how she had transformed his life.

After leaving the CIA, Grant had been led on a journey to become a pastor. While doing so primarily on his own, he never really felt alone along the way, especially given the friendships formed and fellowship experienced while at the seminary. Arriving on the East End of Long Island for his first call as pastor of St. Mary's Lutheran Church in Manorville, his vocation had seemed all consuming, at least for the first six or seven years. But even staying incredibly busy with his congregation, loneliness snuck up and eventually took hold. It wasn't until a bizarre and dangerous set of circumstances brought Jennifer and him together that his loneliness melted away into a kind of love Stephen previously doubted would ever happen for him.

Pastor Charmichael concluded the baptism by declaring "Peace be with you." Sarah, though, was still crying, which generated additional laughter.

The Larson family returned to their pew, and Stephen walked over and sat down in one of the chairs on the side of the altar. Zack did the same, as a parishioner arrived at the lectern to read the morning's lesson from Acts. Zack's strong voice led the congregation in the beautifully written Psalmody, before the reader again stood to share the second reading, which for the Second Sunday of Easter was from 1 Peter 1:3-9. It read in part:

"In this you rejoice, though now for a little while, if necessary, you have been grieved by various trials, so that the tested genuineness of your faith – more precious than gold that perishes though it is tested by fire – may be found to result in praise and glory and honor at the revelation of Jesus Christ."

Stephen listened to the words, with no way of knowing the trials and tests that lay ahead.

Chapter 3

"This was a good day," Jennifer declared. "Pam and Scott's little Sarah being baptized, so many church members attending and the party afterward." She sighed with contentment. "Who would have thought this would happen after the shooting?"

Scott and Pam Larson were integral parts of the St. Mary's family, and in the lives of Jennifer and Stephen. Scott served as the church choir director, and Pam as both the organist and youth director. They were a team. When Scott had been badly injured during a shooting at St. Mary's, the entire church came to their support. And when the two got married, and Pam later was expecting, St. Mary's rejoiced.

"Sarah is a true blessing. And it's not everyday that one of us pastor-types becomes a godfather," Stephen replied. "We get invited to perform the baptisms, not to be a sponsor. I've baptized 123 people, and it's my first stint as a godfather."

"Socks." Jennifer tossed four pairs of black socks across the bed next to Stephen.

"Thanks."

It was Sunday evening. Jennifer and Stephen were packing for a trip to Las Vegas. She was going to speak at a conference at her alma mater, UNLV. Jennifer studied

English Literature as an undergrad there, later coming east to earn a PhD in economics from NYU.

Meanwhile, Stephen would get to visit a friend from seminary whose church in Vegas happened to be hosting a small conference. The plan was to fly out on Tuesday morning, and return early Saturday.

Stephen asked, "Comfortable yet with seeing your father?"

Jennifer's relationship with her father was strained, at best, mainly due to the way he treated – or as Jennifer would point out, mistreated – her late mother. There also were vague questions about her father's dealings as a casino operator for many years. Jennifer never pursued answers to those questions. As she told Stephen a couple of times, "I don't think I want answers. I worry about what I might find. I already have little respect for the man. I've been content with some willful ignorance."

Stephen knew that was a rare state for his wife, so he respected her wishes.

Jennifer answered his question, "I don't think I'll ever be truly comfortable with him. But as you've suggested, maybe this visit will provide an opportunity for some kind of new start."

"I admit that I'm curious to meet my father-in-law face to face. He can't be all bad given that he's your father. I'm certainly impressed how you turned out."

"Well, my love, he had very little to do with that."

Stephen smiled, trying to lighten the conversation a bit. "He's also got that really nice plane."

Jennifer smiled tolerantly at her husband, while shaking her head and continuing to pack her suitcase.

Dixon Shaw's wedding present to his daughter and son-in-law nearly a year ago was a week's honeymoon in Napa Valley, not to mention the ride there and back on his Gulfstream G650. Since she was a child, Jennifer's father tried to make amends through large, ostentatious gifts.

After no communication for nearly two years, that was his way of trying to reach out at their wedding.

Jennifer told Stephen that since discovering in high school that he had cheated on her mom, she never really knew what to do with her anger toward her father, or what to do about his gifts.

Stephen also knew that Jennifer's troubles with her father were only magnified when her first marriage to Ted Brees, once a Long Island congressman and now a U.S. senator, ended due to his affair with his chief of staff.

As her marriage to Brees was falling apart, and before she and Stephen were together, Jennifer had volunteered, "My father wasn't the greatest dad, and as I recognized in high school and college, he was a lousy husband. I found out that he cheated pretty regularly on my mother, on us. When I spoke to her about it, I can remember being so stunned that she knew about it. Yet, she did nothing ... for various reasons. I swore that I would never marry someone like my father. And then I recently discovered that I did."

Months later, when they were alone, Jennifer told Stephen that her mother once said it was important to recognize that marriage was a lifetime commitment. Jennifer added, "I agreed with her. Still do, of course. That becomes much harder, though, when your partner wanders. But to be honest, as I think back, I have this feeling there was more at work. I think she might have been a bit afraid of him, even though my father never, ever raised a hand to either one of us, or gave off the vibe or impression that he would."

Stephen filed that information away in case he needed it one day. He had only spoken to his father-in-law briefly twice on the phone – once before the wedding when Dixon called to say that he could not attend, and a second time after the honeymoon, when Jennifer and Stephen called to say thank you for the generous gift.

Jennifer had not spoken to her father after that post-honeymoon chat for several months. Then she received the invitation to the UNLV conference. She discussed with Stephen whether or not she should let her father know they would be in town. After much angst, Jennifer decided to call, and the result was that they actually would be staying at one of his casino hotels during their visit.

Stephen zipped up his luggage. "Finished. How about you?"

Jennifer folded one more piece of clothing, and deposited it in her suitcase. "I think that's it for me as well. Later, I'll give Joan a call to make sure she can come by just to check the house while we're away."

While Joan and George Kraus were friends of the Grants, as well as church members, Jennifer and Joan were like sisters. In fact, other than Stephen, no one was closer to Jennifer than Joan.

"Good." Stephen moved his suitcase next to the bedroom door, and then returned for Jennifer's. "Allow me." He zipped her suitcase, carried it over and put it down next to his.

Jennifer sat down on the bed. "I couldn't eat dinner after what I had at the party. How about you?"

"No, me either. But I might go for a snack later, if I build up an appetite." He walked over to an oak dresser, and turned on an iPod resting in its dock.

Jennifer tilted her head, crossed her legs, folded her arms, and asked, "Really? And what exactly are you going to do that would build up such an appetite? Maybe work out a little?"

Stephen smiled as the jazz sounds of Amanda Carr, singing with The Kenny Hadley Big Band, began emanating from the speakers. He turned and walked over to Jennifer, replying, "I would not use the phrase 'work out.' But I did have something in mind that would burn up a few calories."

Jennifer lay back on the bed. "Well, let's see what we can do about that appetite then."

Chapter 4

Monday usually was Pastor Grant's day off. But given his travel schedule over the next five days, he would be in the office at St. Mary's this particular Monday.

First, though, was his scheduled early breakfast.

For a few years now, Stephen shared devotions and breakfast on Mondays, Wednesdays and Fridays with his two closest friends – Father Tom Stone and Father Ron McDermott – when their respective schedules allowed. Most times, they met at the Moriches Bay Diner on Montauk Highway. The shiny diner, with its big windows and wide menu, was located just a few minutes from Stephen and Jennifer's home in Center Moriches on Long Island's south shore.

Father McDermott, a priest at St. Luke's Roman Catholic Church and School, was a muscular, stocky five feet six inches, with close-cut blond hair. Stephen appreciated Ron's directness. There was no mistaking where Father McDermott – never Father Ron – stood on a topic. At the same time, though people did not always pick up on it when they first met him, Ron cared deeply about his parishioners, St. Luke's students, the community, his friends, and his church. He would do almost anything for them.

Ron was nearly always found in traditional clerical garb, and that was the case this morning. Stephen, also dressed in his collar, happened to arrive at the same time as Ron. They looked like clergy bookends entering the diner.

Already waiting in a roomy booth was Father Stone, the rector at St. Bartholomew's Anglican Church.

Father Stone and St. Bart's served as an oasis of traditional Christianity contrasted against the relativism and revisionism that had overtaken the U.S. Episcopal Church. Indeed, it was their shared traditional Christian sensibilities, while also acknowledging some inevitable differences, that provided the foundation of the friendship between Stephen, Tom and Ron.

Stone was in his early fifties, having eight years on Grant. Over the past year, under the guidance of his wife, Maggie, Tom had lost some 20 pounds, which noticeably reduced a stomach paunch that had hung on his five-foot-ten-inch frame for a number of years.

Stephen loved Stone's easy laugh and upbeat sense of humor. If the weather was at least 60 degrees, Tom could be found in his off-duty attire of choice – shorts and loud Hawaiian shirts. It was a not-so-subtle reflection of Tom's attitude on life. So, on this warm, spring day, Tom was brandishing a blue shirt with rather large palm trees.

Finally, another pastor sat at the table. In recent months, this ecumenical breakfast trio had been extended to a foursome with the inclusion of Zack Charmichael. Zack, who became the assistant pastor at St. Mary's about ten months prior, was in his late twenties, and gave off a gangly, young vibe with thick, unkempt, light brown hair and dark, rectangular glasses, sitting atop a very thin five-feet-seven-inches. Stephen thought that Zack and Tom, despite the difference in age, were rather similar in their outlook on life. They were, for the most part, positive men with a penchant for enthusiasm.

Stephen also found it interesting, and perhaps a bit telling, that Tom's oldest daughter, Cara, and Zack had been dating for a few months now.

After the four men finished their readings and prayers from *For All the Saints: A Prayer Book For and By the Church*, the waitress arrived with their breakfast orders.

Ron looked across the table at Tom's breakfast. "I have to hand it to you, Tom. If someone had told me a year ago that you'd be eating Cheerios and fruit for breakfast, I would have said that person was nuts."

"And notice it's not Frosted Cheerios. It's all about making choices, my friend, and having the will power to carry them out," replied Tom, smiling at his own exaggeration as he splashed skim milk on O-shaped whole grain oats.

Sitting directly across from Tom, Stephen chimed in, "Right, and there's also the fact that Maggie laid down the dietary law, and gave you no real choice."

Zack laughed a bit louder with that comment.

"Ridiculous. To quote Ralph Kramden, I am the king of my castle." Tom usually chuckled at his own jokes, and did so this time. He turned to look at Zack sitting next to him, pointed a spoon, and added, "And you're not going to tell Maggie or Cara about my king-of-the-castle crack, right?"

Zack's smile was reined in to a mere smirk, and then he bit into a breakfast quesadilla.

Ron observed, "How brave, not to mention abusing the power of the future father-in-law."

"Father-in-law?" Tom shot looks at Ron and then Zack, who while chewing, raised his hands in innocence and shook his head.

Zack swallowed and protested, "Hey, I didn't say it. Ron did."

Tom took a mouthful of cereal. He finished chewing and then added, "I am not ready for my little girl to get married." He paused. "But I suppose she could do worse than you."

"Well, thanks, I think?"

Tom added, "If you ever do ask for Cara's hand, you better come to me first."

Zack deflected, "Okay, can we talk about something else, please?"

Stephen decided to bail out his young friend. "So, anything more interesting this week than a trip to Vegas?"

As he spread cream cheese on a toasted cinnamon-raisin bagel, Ron replied, "I've learned never to declare that my week is going to be more exciting than Stephen Grant's."

Grant's three friends knew that he had been a SEAL and with the CIA, though they of course were unaware of the lengths to which Grant had gone in protecting his country and fellow Americans. But they more recently had seen their friend in action in rare, unique situations whereby Grant was forced to be a bit more warrior than clergy.

Ron continued, "Remind me, again, why are you heading to Las Vegas?"

"Jen is speaking at her alma mater, UNLV, as part of a conference on the state of economic freedom around the world."

Zack chimed in, "Not sure about elsewhere, but I can confidently say that economic freedom is suffering right here at home."

"Agreed," added Ron.

"Thanks, I'll let Jen know that you two are in agreement," barbed Stephen.

"You're welcome," replied Ron.

"Anyway, it turns out that a friend from seminary who has a church in Vegas is hosting a small conference as well. It's about immigration and the church. He was at my wedding, Pastor Jacob Stout."

Tom confirmed, "Big Jake, retired high school football coach. Right?"

"Yes, good memory."

"We had a chance to talk some football that day. Seemed like a good guy."

"He is."

Tom added, "In college and a bit after, my friends and I used to pop over to Vegas now and then. That was the late seventies, early eighties. Haven't been back there since. Things have changed quite a bit from what I understand." Stone spent his high school and college years in southern California.

Ron declared, "I've never been there."

"That does not surprise me," replied Stephen with a smile. "Just can't see Father McDermott in Sin City."

Ron replied, "Darn right, you can't."

"I actually was there three years ago for the Consumer Electronics Show," volunteered Zack.

"That doesn't surprise me, either. I would be rather disappointed if the biggest nerd – and I use that word with utmost affection – I know had never been to the largest electronics show." Stephen poured some additional syrup on his French toast.

Zack was a nerd in a very tech-savvy, video-gaming, comic-book-loving kind of way.

"Hey, I'm proud of my nerdist leanings," Zack replied. He tilted his head down to highlight the fact that he was wearing a t-shirt with Green Lantern's logo emblazoned on the front. "As for Vegas, though, I didn't see much of the city, and certainly didn't gamble. It was all about the tech for a few days."

Stephen added, "I haven't been to Vegas since my CIA days, but..."

Tom interrupted, "Ah, tuxedo, beautiful women, a martini, baccarat and an over-the-top bad guy."

Stephen chuckled. "Of course. This is sort of a trip home for Jen. It's where she grew up." He left it there, without getting into her angst about returning to see her father.

Ron reflected, "It's got to be tough having a parish in Las Vegas with all the temptations around."

Stephen replied, "Perhaps, although temptation is everywhere, right?"

Tom said, "Most people are surprised to learn that there's no prohibition against gambling in the Bible. Gambling is not dealt with directly in Scripture."

Stephen noted, "It comes down to questions of what gambling could lead to – stewardship issues, greed, envy, possible addiction."

"But those warnings apply to all kinds of activities, not just gambling," injected Tom.

"I agree," responded Stephen. "I've always looked at gambling as an activity that ranks as an enjoyable diversion or form of entertainment for some, while a real or potential problem for others. Is there a difference between a well-off grandmother who sets aside a small part of her income to visit Atlantic City each month, and an out-of-work father using the few family bucks set aside for an emergency to buy Powerball tickets? Absolutely. Then there's more of an academic question of what's truly gambling. Is gambling just about games of chance, such as a lottery? Or, does it include games of strategy, like poker and even horse racing, where strategy, experience and even math come into play?"

"I don't think most people think about those distinctions, especially our Christian brethren who declare all gambling to be a sin," answered Tom.

Zack volunteered, "Well, you know, growing up, my family always emphasized the evils of gambling. In my house, gambling was a sin, plain and simple."

Stephen replied, "Really? What about you today?"

"I understand that we can't label something a sin that the Bible doesn't say is a sin."

Stephen said, "Jesus warned against 'teaching as doctrines the commandments of men.'"

Ron added, "Ah, Matthew 15:9. God gave us brains to discern and judge."

Tom smiled. "Like should a Catholic Church run bingo games or not, right, Ron?"

"Don't get me started. You know we don't do that at St. Luke's, and quite frankly, fewer and fewer Catholic churches do the bingo thing."

Stephen looked at Tom, "Couldn't resist, could you? Had to tweak him."

"Naturally," said Tom.

"No worries, Stephen," said Ron. "How could I let *his* childish comments bother me?"

Tom laughed. "I don't know how you could, but I think my comments get to you pretty often."

Ron replied, "Not for the reasons you think. It just pains me to have a friend who exhibits such lame attempts at humor."

Stephen enjoyed these exchanges between Ron and Tom. In several ways, they were very different men, yet Stephen knew they were best of friends, would do anything for each other, and that this verbal sparring had become a fun part of their relationship.

Zack refocused the conversation. "Anyway, my family – specifically, my grandfather – had a hard experience with what the greed and the wild risks in pursuit of the big payoff can do to a person, and those who love him. I didn't see it firsthand, but my father reminded us regularly. So, other than things like our friendly non-money bets that you and I have on football and baseball games, Stephen, I try to stay away from the gambling thing."

Stephen nodded. "Okay, I didn't know any of that."

Zack replied, "Hey, I keep it low key. I don't play the holier-than-the-Bible bit on gambling. I've seen that in other areas, and it bugs me. It's like the deal on video gaming. There are plenty of Christians who see nothing but evil in video games. They can't distinguish between different games and legitimate individual differences as to what might be a risk for a few but not for most. Part of that's a generational thing, I think. Many of the people condemning video games tend to be older folks who have never played a video game in their lives."

"I can see that point," observed Tom.

"Coming from an older folk who has never played a video game, right, Tom?" observed Stephen.

Tom replied, "Thanks for that. You're a riot."

Ron added, "My concerns about Las Vegas go beyond the gambling. It's about other activities that raise clear moral objections. And then there's that whole mob thing."

Zack asked, "Mob thing?"

"Yes, you know, organized crime involved in running casinos and the city."

Zack replied, "Really? I thought we were talking about twenty-first-century Las Vegas, not the 1950s or the Sixties."

Chapter 5

After what was assumed to be a busy and profitable weekend, the new workweek began with a Monday lunch at one of the Las Vegas casinos controlled by Dixon Shaw.

It was held in Dix's personal penthouse suite at the Casino Beach Vegas Resort. The 6,600-square-foot, two-story penthouse featured a master suite and two additional smaller suites, each with deep soaking tubs; dining room and gourmet kitchen; office and conference room; living room with fireplace; game room with billiards and poker tables (a dealer on call); movie theater; balcony Jacuzzi, waterfall and pool; and floor-to-ceiling windows throughout overlooking the city and beyond.

Among the attendees at the Monday lunch were Shaw's chief operating officer and right hand man, Nicky Geraci, and his chief financial officer, Chet Easton. Geraci and Easton also were minority partners in Shaw's growing casino empire, which included Casino Beach and The Twenties Club and Casino, with The River Park and Resort under construction.

Easton looked the part of a respectable CFO for a major business concern, dressed in a dark suit with a vest. The man was in his late fifties, thin, short and bald, with silver, wire-rimmed glasses resting on a large nose. His face easily lent itself to a scowl. Easton gave the impression of always calculating. He rarely spoke, but when doing so, a nasally tone seemed to fit perfectly.

The executive directors of Dix's casinos – Lou Hammett for The Twenties and Martina Petty for Casino Beach – also attended. Compared to others in the room, Hammett looked like he was barely out of college. He was a tall 31-year-old, with a long, large head and short brown hair. But he was chubby, and that chubbiness made him look several years younger. Hammett was smart, including a Wharton MBA, friendly, and seemed to know every management theory on how to motivate people. Everyone loved working for Lou Hammett.

Meanwhile, Petty was a petite blond, always dressed to perfection in the latest style, and possessing a fierce competence and an attention to detail that she demanded from everyone around her. Martina Petty's employees were motivated as well, but it was out of a combination of being highly compensated, and living in fear of making a mistake. Compared to Hammett, Petty's management style was simple and direct: You're paid handsomely, so do your job, or lose it. The 40-year-old did not suffer fools well. The Casino Beach specialized in putting guests at ease by making them feel like they were on a beach with nearly every luxury and gaming option at their fingertips, and Petty ran the casino by making sure the people who worked for her rarely felt at ease. Few on staff missed the irony.

Dix finished the last bite of his seared Mahi Mahi.

Petty nodded curtly, and three staff members cleared away everyone's lunch plates, and replaced them with a dessert of Haupia Macadamia Nut Bread Pudding.

Dix took a bite of the croissant, coconut, and macadamia creation, and smiled at Martina. "Excellent, as always. But I'll need a few more minutes in the gym."

Martina nodded in response.

Shaw was in his early sixties. But there was little evidence of time taking much of a toll, except perhaps for the salt-and-pepper color of his tight, neatly cut hair, which, in fact, only served to amplify an intoxicating charm. At a formidable six-foot-two, he was tanned, fit, energetic and quick-witted.

Dix said, "All right then, you have the schedules for when these four candidates for the The River exec position will be in town. As I said, I want each of you to show them around. Make clear what we're about, and determine if they would fit with us and with our culture. Good?"

All four responded with varying signals of agreement.

"The only other item that you need to be aware of on my end is that my daughter and son-in-law will be in town for part of the week. So, I probably will not be making my full rounds." Shaw made a point of circulating throughout each casino on a regular basis, especially to make the high rollers feel welcome and at home.

Hammett smiled. "That's great, Dix. I look forward to meeting your family."

"Thanks, Lou."

Martina quickly and uncomfortably added, "As do I, sir."

"Of course, and thank you, Martina." He paused, and then announced, "Well, that's all for this Monday meeting, people. Now, let's go make our guests happy."

As Lou and Martina were leaving, Candy Welles emerged from the master suite in the smallest of red bikinis, with her long brunette hair falling gently on her shoulders and back. The 28-year-old beauty and Dix had become nearly inseparable over the past few months. She smiled brightly at everyone, with Dix, Nicky and Chet still seated at the conference table. She leaned down, kissed Dix, and said, "You're joining me in the Jacuzzi, Dix honey?"

"I most surely will, Candy. Just give me a few minutes to wrap up with Chet and Nicky."

Dix watched as she walked out onto the balcony, into the pool and under the waterfall. He turned back to his partners. "Gentlemen, I obviously have better things to do than sit here with you." As his eyes returned from also watching Candy, Geraci commented, "You certainly do."

Easton said, "Dix, I want to come back to the idea of going public. Why not ...?"

Shaw interrupted, "Chet, we've been through this. I know where you are. But I see no reason to go public. We're well funded, growing, and I see no reason to get involved with all of the added costs and regulations that come with being a publicly traded company."

"But what about ...?"

Shaw stepped on Easton once more. "Look, the three of us are making plenty of money – I'm guessing more than any of us imagined we would during our lifetimes – and I'm fully confident that with The River coming soon, we're going to make a hell of a lot more. And that's not even counting our getting ready for online opportunities."

Easton sighed, and looked at Geraci, who offered no tells as to where he stood on the matter.

With resignation in his voice, Easton said, "It's the wrong call, Dix."

"But it's my call to make, Chet," said Shaw. "And now gentlemen, if you'll excuse me, I have an appointment with Ms. Welles."

As the two men entered the elevator, Easton said, "Well, that's that with Dix on going public."

Geraci replied, "We already knew that, didn't we? That really wasn't necessary." He pulled on each tan glove, which nicely matched his tan, summer-weight suit.

"Just making sure."

As the elevator doors closed, Geraci and Easton could see Shaw in the distance descending into the Jacuzzi where Candy waited.

Easton asked, "Do you think he's going to marry Candy?"

Geraci smiled. "He didn't marry the others. I don't think we have to worry about a Mrs. Candy Shaw."

"I certainly hope not."

Chapter 6

The taxi ride from McCarran International Airport to The Twenties was less than eight miles. It took a few minutes longer than normal, though, as Jennifer asked the driver to take the Strip – or Las Vegas Boulevard South – rather than scooting along the Las Vegas Freeway.

As they drove past the landmark "Welcome to Fabulous Las Vegas Nevada" sign, Jennifer squeezed Stephen's hand. "I love that sign."

Stephen was a bit surprised. "Really?"

"It's one of the very few things around here that hasn't changed since I was a kid."

"Isn't Vegas all about change, my economist wife?"

She nodded. "The change here just since I was growing up is incredible. I don't think people from many other parts of the country fully get it. But when you live it, it's actually kind of natural. In fact, living it was one of the things that led me into economics." She turned from her husband, and looked out the window. "Still, no one ever said change was always easy."

Stephen joined Jennifer in looking out at casinos and hotels of wildly different shapes and sizes – from the Luxor's Great Sphinx and pyramid to the MGM Grand's golden lion, along with the "Eiffel Tower Experience" at Paris Las Vegas. While Stephen had been to Las Vegas a few times, the last visit had come more than fifteen years ago – long predating Jennifer, his becoming a pastor, and a chunk of what he was now seeing.

Stephen turned to Jennifer. "Can I tell you something?"

"Of course."

"I've never been able to fully fit you and Las Vegas together. And now that you and I are here, I still really can't."

Jennifer smiled. "There's more to Vegas than the Strip and gambling. While I was growing up, even with my father in the casino business, my parents, especially my mom, tried to keep me away from much of it. Many people here have little to do with gambling, and only wind up on the Strip when giving the tour to relatives visiting from out of town. At the same time, though, it's hard not to be influenced. So much of recreational and cultural life occurs at or around the casinos. And let's face it, few would be here without gambling. But all in all, my childhood was pretty normal, at least until I hit late high school."

"I know..."

"And there's still a good deal of Las Vegas in this girl of yours." She leaned over and kissed him. "That includes some Vegas heat."

"One of my favorite parts."

The taxi pulled up to the front doors of The Twenties Club and Casino. The massive building was an amalgamation of 1920s-era architecture. At the street level, the building offered large, two-story arches, red brick, and clear windows. Above the arches, a huge retro-neon sign proclaimed "The Twenties Club and Casino." As one's eyes ascended further, the red brick gave way to an art-deco look, with stainless steel, chrome, and stained glass arranged in symmetrical, geometric forms. Crowning the top of the building was a replica of the upper floors and spear of New York City's Chrysler Building.

The door of the taxi was opened by a young man dressed in a burgundy, white-striped blazer, white oxford shirt with a blue bow tie, pleated, ivory trousers, and white buck wingtips. "Welcome to The Twenties," he announced with a smile.

After Jennifer and Stephen got out of the taxi, Lou Hammett stepped forward, and said, "Pastor and Dr. Grant, I'm so pleased to meet you. I'm Lou Hammett, the executive director here at The Twenties." After exchanging quick pleasantries, Hammett turned and gave instructions to his staff to take care of the Grants' luggage.

Following Hammett down the stairs was Dixon Shaw. "Jenny, I'm so happy to see you."

As Shaw gave Jennifer a hug, Stephen could see his wife tense up. He also heard the unease in her voice, when she said, "Hi, Dad, how are you?"

Stephen understood how out of character this was. It was the most rare of occasions when Jennifer failed to be engaging and welcoming. She was adept at making others feel at ease. Watching Dixon Shaw, Stephen actually saw the same traits in her father. *I guess you'd need that running a casino.*

Jennifer's father turned to Stephen, "Pastor, it's about time we met face to face."

Stephen said, "Mr. Shaw, it's a pleasure..."

Shaw interrupted with a laugh. "'Mr. Shaw'? Come on. It's Dix."

"Of course, Dix, and it's Stephen."

Shaw replied, "If you don't mind, can I stick with 'Pastor'? It makes me feel better when I worry about my Jenny, knowing that she is being taken care of not only by a man of the cloth, but one who knows how to handle himself in a time of danger." Stephen knew that Dix was referring to the shooting that occurred at St. Mary's before Jen and Stephen were married. Dix lowered his voice. "And former CIA to boot. You sure as hell are a vast improvement over that asshole politician Ted Brees. How did that sleazy bastard become a U.S. senator? But then again, it's politics, right? After I found out what he did, I was going to..."

Jennifer, with a hint of daughter-like scolding in her voice, said, "Dad, please."

Stephen pondered what Dixon Shaw might do to Ted Brees, and part of him was okay with it. He also picked up the slight shrug of the shoulders and pleading eyes directed his way by Jennifer.

Shaw's smile broadened a bit more. "Sorry, Jenny."

Stephen saw Dix enjoying his daughter, and thought it appeared genuine. Stephen even picked up a bit of tension draining from Jennifer.

A small, gentle clearing of the throat came from behind Shaw.

He turned, "Baby, I'm so sorry." He took Candy Welles' hand and brought her forward. "Jenny and Pastor, this is Candy Welles, the beautiful light in my life."

Stephen extended his hand. "Of course, we've met Ms. Welles before. It's good to see you."

Jennifer seemed taken off guard. "Well, yes, hello, Ms. Welles."

"I wasn't sure if you'd remember me," Candy replied.

"As the flight attendant on Dix's Casino Beach jet on our wedding night, it would be hard to forget," answered Stephen.

"You certainly had more interesting things to be focused on that night, but that's so nice. And please, call me Candy. It's like we're almost family."

Jennifer replied, "Um, family? Yes, well, Candy it is."

Dix added, "It was shortly after that flight that we started seeing each other."

Jennifer observed, "How nice."

Stephen could see Jennifer's emotional conflict. *Move things in a different direction, Grant, and quickly.* He looked around, and said, "The Twenties looks like an intriguing resort."

As he slid his arm around Candy's waist, Dix replied, "I'm very proud of it, and of the work being done by Lou. How about a quick tour, then you two can settle in a bit and we'll have dinner later?" Looking at Stephen, Dix added, "I thought you could meet my business partners."

"That sounds great to me," answered Stephen. "How about you, Jen?"

She answered slowly, "Yes, of course. But I already know Nicky and Chet."

Dix commented, "But you've never seen The Twenties, have you, Jenny?"

"No, Dad, I haven't."

Dix nodded at Hammett, who was standing off to the side. "Lou, give us the grand tour."

"Yes, sir, Dix," said Hammett. He signaled over a waitress, who was wearing a short flapper dress with sequins and dangling fringes, a long strand of pearls, bobbed hair, and a cloche hat. She presented a tray of champagne flutes. Jennifer was the first to take a glass, followed by Candy, Stephen and Dix.

Dix toasted the arrival of his daughter and son-in-law, and they all took a sip of the 1995 Krug Clos d'Ambonnay.

As the small group turned to follow Lou, Jennifer whispered in Stephen's ear, "I'll be needing a few more of these, I think."

Lou, along with Dix and Candy, took Stephen and Jennifer on a nearly hour-long stroll throughout the massive hotel, including the Speakeasy Lounge that featured various musical and comedy acts. The Round Table was the resort's top-tiered restaurant, fashioned after and saluting The Algonquin Round Table of Dorothy Parker fame. Harlem Jazz served up some of the best music in all of Vegas. The two casinos in the building had different personalities – Prohibition sought to capture a 1920s Chicago feel, while the Miami Deal served up palm trees and a large windmill in the middle of the room as a tip to the Roman Pools & Casino of 1920s Miami. The tour went on to include pools, dozens of shops, a spa and salon, fitness center, art gallery, and a small arena.

The tour ended at the door of the suite that Dix insisted Stephen and Jennifer stay in as his guests.

In response to protests from both Jennifer and Stephen, Dix declared, "A beautiful suite for a few days, as my guests, is the very least that this negligent father, not to mention negligent father-in-law, can do."

He kissed Jennifer on the cheek, slapped Stephen on the back, took Candy's hand, and walked away.

While heading down the hall, Dix said over his shoulder, "We'll see you at dinner. Nine o'clock in the Speakeasy."

Chapter 7

After entering the suite, Stephen gave a little whistle of admiration. "This is rather nice."

The marble foyer fed into a spacious living room.

A bedroom with a king-sized bed had a sliding door into a bathroom that included a steam shower and deep whirlpool tub. Both the living room and bedroom offered widescreen televisions, and huge windows with broad views of Las Vegas. Throughout, the furniture had an elegant, formal appearance, but as Stephen tested the sofa and the bed, he discovered deep comfort as well.

But what drew his attention were the telephones in each room. A replica brushed-chrome candlestick phone, with the earpiece hanging on a hook, sat on a table in the living room, while a black, brass-trimmed, antique desktop telephone, featuring a cradle-top handset, could be found on a nightstand in the bedroom. The only differences from nine decades earlier, when such phones were normally in use, were the push buttons rather than the rotary dialing.

"These phones are great, aren't they?" observed Stephen.

Jennifer smiled and shook her head. "The telephones?"

"What?"

She spread her arms. "You've got this suite with all kinds of amenities, and you focus on the telephones?"

"Well, aren't they cool?" He also smiled.

Jennifer examined the candlestick phone closer. "Okay, I do like the phones."

"Hah, I knew you would."

"Sometimes you're such an idiot."

"But you love me anyway."

"Yes, I do," she acknowledged with mock reluctance.

Stephen sat down on the couch and looked at what was arranged on the coffee table. "Well, your father or Mr. Hammett has provided a German Riesling and a Gouda from Holland – nice pairing." He held up the bottle. "Did you mean it before when you whispered the need for more to drink?"

Jennifer smirked, and then declared, "You know what, if I'm having dinner tonight with my father, along with his latest very young girlfriend and old cronies, then I will have a glass."

Stephen started to ease the cork out of the bottle. "Tsk, tsk, drinking your family troubles away. But then again, this is Vegas."

Jennifer came over and sat next to him. As Stephen poured two glasses, Jennifer instructed, "Open up." She deposited a piece of the cheese in his mouth, and took a bite herself.

They both sipped the wine.

"How is it that you know so much about wine and cheese pairings?" she asked.

"It's from my days with the agency. You know, there actually were a few James Bond-like moments, and ..."

Jennifer joked, "Stop. I should have known better than to ask."

Stephen laughed. *Actually, there were a few.* He said, "Hey, I could have said that many clergy know their wines."

"Big difference between picking a wine for communion, and understanding which wine goes with which cheese."

"You're right about that. The Riesling stands up well to the cheese. In fact, the fruity, sweet flavors in the cheese are truly enhanced by this full-bodied wine. Don't you think?"

"I happen to know that you're not nearly as pompous as you sound."

"Thanks, I think?"

Jennifer paused, and then moved a hand to Stephen's cheek. "You know, there is at least one thing upon which my father and I agree."

"And what's that?"

"He feels better that I'm with a man like you."

They kissed gently.

Jennifer walked over to the floor-to-ceiling window, and looked down on her hometown of Las Vegas.

Stephen asked, "What are you thinking about?"

"After not seeing my father for so long, it's always the same. I'm reminded of how perplexing he is."

"Why perplexing?"

"You saw how charming he can be."

"No doubt," responded Stephen, as he took another sip of the Riesling.

"Did you get the impression that he and Candy were really in love, or at least something close?"

"Actually, that's what I was picking up."

"He's been that way throughout my life. He was like that with my mom, even after I found out that he was cheating. And since she died, I've now seen him with three different women, and he's been the same way with each. I meet a new woman. He seems to be in love. And then when I see him a few years later, there's a new woman. And judging by Candy, they're getting younger." She took a large gulp of the wine.

"What about how he treats you? He looked really happy. In fact, Dix lit up talking with you."

"My father has always treated me the same, as a kind of princess. In fact, if it wasn't for the way he treated mom, I'd probably still be as infatuated with my dad as I was growing up."

"But?"

"You say he lit up with me. But how genuine is that? I mean, he appeared to love my mom, and look at what he did. And how could he not realize that cheating on his wife would hurt his daughter as well?"

Stephen swallowed another piece of the Gouda. "That's not unusual. I can't tell you how many times I've heard even the spouses who were cheated on say about their cheating spouse, or ex, 'He's a good father, just a bad husband.' Or, 'She's a great mom, just an unfaithful wife.' They compartmentalize."

"Believe me, I know firsthand. Mom even said that about my father after I found out about his philandering. But it's a total package. He didn't just cheat on her, he cheated on me, on our family."

"I never asked before, but did you ever talk to him about this?"

"Early on, I tried. But he just couldn't seem to grasp what I was saying, or didn't want to. I think he assumed I would come around to his way of looking at the entire thing."

How to put this? After a pause, Stephen said, "Given his charm and obvious skills as a compartmentalizer, I can understand being perplexed. But that compartmentalizing could well mean, and probably does, that his love for you is quite genuine, no matter its obvious blind spots. So, in the end, the big question is: What kind of relationship do you want with Dix?"

"Thanks for that," Jennifer answered sarcastically.

"You're welcome. That's what I'm here for, those penetrating insights."

Jennifer sighed. "I might not know what kind of relationship I want with Dixon Shaw, but I do know that I'll have some more wine." She sat down next to him once again.

As he poured, Stephen said, "You know what this reminds me of?"

"No, what?"

"Well, the period-style décor, and us drinking a nice wine..."

Jen laughed.

"What?" Stephen protested.

"You're going to have an Irene Dunne moment." She smiled. "And thank you. Whenever you mention that I remind you of a Hollywood starlet, how can I help but be flattered?"

From the earliest moments of their relationship – in fact, even before they got together – Stephen thought that Jen had much in common with the classic film actress Irene Dunne. The two shared sharp facial features, a slightly upturned nose, a thin build, short hair, and perhaps most unique, a voice with ironic upper-class, playful, and seductive inflections.

Jennifer added, "Besides, I know how that brain of yours works when it comes to movies and life, even if I don't necessarily understand it."

"Don't understand it, hmmm?"

Jennifer whispered, "Not in the least."

They kissed once more.

Chapter 8

On stage, the Speakeasy Lounge was about to leave the 1920s behind, in favor of the Rat Pack's Las Vegas of the early 1960s. But in terms of ambiance, the place had the timeless feel of a top-tier steak house that could be operating in 1925, in 1965 or in the twenty-first century.

Large tables covered with white linen; deep, dark leather chairs and benches; and waiters and waitresses sporting white shirts, bow ties, and vests set the mood. Each staff member also displayed vast knowledge not only of steak, but also of all the other food dishes on the menu, as well as the "Prohibition Lawbreakers" list of drinks from the 1920s, including the Southside, the Sidecar, a Mary Pickford, the Ward 8, the Bee's Knees and a Highball.

"Dix, that was one of the best steaks I've ever had." Stephen was not exaggerating for the sake of his father-in-law. His 10-ounce, herb crusted filet mignon seemed to melt in his mouth.

"I'm glad you enjoyed it, Pastor. What about your veal tenderloin medallions, Jenny?"

"Delicious, especially with the mushrooms."

The assessments of respective meals continued around the table, to Candy and her steak-and-chicken Cobb Salad, Nicky Geraci's marinated and grilled T-bone, Chet Easton's Brazilian flank steak with a salsa sauce, and steak au poivre for Chet's wife, Angelica.

Given that old habits die hard, or don't truly die at all, Stephen assessed each person at the table, similar to evaluating individuals or groups he met while at the CIA.

His initial impressions of Dix as smooth, skilled with people, and extremely comfortable in his own skin were reinforced, as was his assessment of Candy being both sweet and a touch manipulative.

Stephen had to work to stop his eyes from wandering back to the gloved hands of Nicky Geraci. *What's the story there?* Stephen, however, could easily peg other aspects of Geraci's tale, noting that Geraci was always watching and listening to those at the table, as well as to those around the rest of the room. While Geraci was introduced as chief operating officer of Shaw's casino business, Stephen knew protection and security when he saw it. The unmistakable vibe picked up by Grant was that Nicky Geraci was primarily Dix's muscle.

Muscle? Interesting word selection, Grant. Very Vegas.

Meanwhile, Chet didn't say much. But while Geraci was on the job looking for security threats, Stephen thought Easton was busy tallying up the dinner bill. He oozed accountant, or even bookkeeper – though extremely well paid, no doubt.

The contrast between Chet and Angelica, though, was almost comical. While Chet was thin, short and bald, and rather nondescript in his dark suit, his wife was four inches taller and many inches wider, while magnifying her presence further with brunette hair in a beehive; a bright yellow, almost prom-like dress; and a loud, grating voice.

After Angelica declared disappointment with her steak, she and Chet engaged in a discussion that Chet clearly was looking to keep quiet and preferably end quickly. But his wife appeared uninterested or incapable of doing either.

As the little marital spat wound down, Dix shifted the conversation for the others at the table. "How goes the economics work, Jenny?"

Jennifer replied, "The business is doing pretty well, Dad. We've got a solid client base, and been doing work on the corporate and policy fronts, not to mention assorted speaking opportunities, including the speech at UNLV on Thursday."

Dix replied, "Back at the alma mater. That should be interesting, right?"

Jennifer answered, "I'm looking forward to it."

"If I've never said it before, I'm very proud of you, Jenny, and what you've accomplished."

Jennifer paused, raised an eyebrow, and looked a bit bewildered at her father.

Dix turned to Stephen. "You know, when she went off to get a PhD in economics in New York, I thought I'd be able to lure her back here when she finished to help run the family business."

Before Stephen could reply, Jennifer said, "Not that I would have, but you never told me that."

Dix nodded, looked at his daughter, and replied, "I know, unfortunately."

Again, Stephen saw that Jen was taken off guard.

Stephen injected, "Well, I'm certainly pleased that she didn't come back, and instead stayed in New York."

Dix looked Stephen in the eye. "I can see that you are, Pastor."

He's good. But sincere?

Shaw then shifted a bit and chuckled. "I think Nicky and Chet also are pleased that Jennifer isn't here. As a result, they get to run much of the show."

Geraci laughed. "Please, like you actually let Chet or I run much." He looked at Jennifer. "All I can say is that it's clear that working with you, Jennifer, would have meant working with the far more respectable part of the Shaw family."

Nicky raised his bourbon-and-ginger-beer Highball and clinked glasses with Jen's Mary Pickford, a mix of rum, pineapple juice, maraschino liqueur and grenadine.

Jennifer smiled. "Thanks, Nicky. I think you're probably right."

Stephen spotted a passing twinge of regret on Jennifer's face, but couldn't detect any reaction from Dix to his daughter's small, though not-too-subtle jab.

Jennifer quickly followed up. "How are things on the ground in the Vegas economy, Dad?"

Dix answered, "We survived the big downturn better than many around here. And while things seem to be turning in Vegas, we're ahead of the curve. Nicky and Chet think we should go public, but we're well positioned. We managed to get great terms financing The River..."

Stephen asked, "Excuse me, River?"

"Yes, The River Park and Resort. It's the next project we're building – a spectacular, exciting mix of casino, dining, entertainment, sports, amusement park, and adventure experience."

Stephen commented, "Sounds interesting."

Dix looked at Stephen and then Jennifer, "If you two have any extra time, I'd love to show you how far along The River is."

"Maybe we can do that. I wouldn't mind seeing what you've done with Casino Beach as well."

Dix said, "Good. Let me know when, and I'll arrange things. We're trying to find an executive director for The River right now. Now, that would be an ideal job for Jenny."

Before Jennifer could reply to another surprise from her father, the waiter arrived for dessert orders, and the conversation subsequently moved to backgrounds.

Stephen discovered that Dix and Nicky had spent their entire careers together in the Las Vegas casino industry, dating back to being teenagers in the 1960s.

Angelica seemed fascinated to hear that Grant was with the CIA, even though he indicated that "most of the work" was rather dull research. She also appeared quite bewildered by his decision to become a pastor.

Stephen, though, was most pleased to get a previously unknown tidbit of information about Jen's childhood. Dix revealed that his daughter in her tween and teen years had a major crush on Robert Urich. He volunteered, "She was addicted to watching 'Spenser: For Hire,' and then she found 'Vega$' from the late seventies on VHS."

Stephen said, "That's fascinating, Dix." He looked mischievously at Jennifer, who frowned in return.

The conversation ended, as the lights dimmed around the room. A man came to the microphone, welcomed everyone, and then announced, "Ladies and gentlemen, it's time for the biggest stars on The Strip. 'The Summit Returns: A Rat Pack Salute.' Enjoy!" He stepped aside, and the spotlight focused on a Frank Sinatra impersonator who kicked things off with "You Make Me Feel So Young."

A lover of swing and big band, Stephen could not help but start to tap his foot. *That's actually not a bad Sinatra.*

Following on stage came faux Dean Martin, Sammy Davis Jr., Joey Bishop and even Peter Lawford. The drink cart, for which the actual Rat Pack was famous, or infamous, for having on stage, came rolling out as well. Stephen assumed the alcohol wasn't real. *But this is Vegas, never know.*

The politically incorrect jokes and ribbing ensued, along with a wide array of Rat Pack songs.

At a small table in the back of the room, a man sat alone. He had eaten a full meal, and was now nursing a beer. At first glance, he seemed to be watching the show, like everyone else in the Speakeasy. But his attention actually was not on Frank, Dino and Sammy. Rather, Gil Rice watched the table where Dixon Shaw was serving as host.

The show eventually closed with Sinatra explaining to the audience what it meant to do it "My Way."

Chapter 9

Given the length of the day on Tuesday, Jennifer and Stephen might have been excused for sleeping a bit later than normal on Wednesday. But they decided to clear out their respective cobwebs with an early morning swim in one of the hotel pools.

After a shower, Jennifer dressed for the first day of her conference in a light gray skirt, matching blazer, and a white blouse. She slipped her MacBook Air into a slim briefcase, and checked the power on her phone. "Okay, I'm set. Since I won't be back until late, have you decided on your schedule for the day, or are you winging it?"

Stephen said, "I don't know. There's a lot to do in Vegas for a guy on his own. I might get into some trouble."

"Should I be worried about your being cut loose in Sin City, *Pastor* Grant? It's too bad the conference at Big Jake's church doesn't start until tomorrow."

Stephen relished the trust they shared. "Hey, I was with the CIA, you know."

"Well, try not to create any international incidents. Why don't you take my father up on his invitation to play in one of the Texas Hold 'Em tournaments?"

"That's what I was thinking actually. Maybe one of the early starts. See how long I might last."

"Given your CIA-acquired skills at pegging people and their true intentions, I should be worried for your opponents."

"You make me sound rather formidable. How did you acquire this knowledge?"

Jennifer raised an eyebrow. "Stephen, my love, I know you, but I'm also smart enough to know what I don't know about you."

Stephen played dumb. "You lost me. You know what you don't know? Are you channeling Donald Rumsfeld, or disputing him?"

"Oh, shut up and kiss me."

Stephen obliged.

As Jennifer turned to leave the suite, Stephen added, "Hey, we haven't talked about what you're thinking regarding dear old dad after yesterday. Seems like he surprised you at times."

"He did. But that will have to wait until tonight," she replied, heading to the door.

"We'll have to talk about Dan Tanna, too. And you claimed not to understand my movie thing. Now I know why you drive that red Thunderbird convertible."

Jennifer laughed, and turned with the smile that he loved. "You've finally figured it out. Enjoy the day, whatever you wind up doing." And Jennifer was gone.

So, Grant, a poker tournament in Las Vegas? What would some of the parishioners at St. Mary's say? And what about your old agency colleagues, given how the last poker tournament you played in turned out? Wow, nearly twenty years ago. A $60 buy-in game is as crazy and high-stakes as it's going to get this time.

The 11:00 AM tournament was scheduled to start with 24 players at three tables. Each person's $60 buy-in translated into $6,000 in tournament chips.

Grant arrived early in the Miami Deal poker room. His table, with a palm tree draped over it, was near the massive windmill. He decided to have some fun by playing a bit looser than he otherwise might. But his instinct to evaluate was not to be suppressed. As each player came to the table, Grant began sizing them up for potential strengths, weaknesses and tells.

A tournament entrant seated at one of the other tables took notice of Grant. He watched as Stephen turned to his right and left, greeting other players. Grant had his back to the man. But when Grant's head turned a bit further in response to a waitress, the man jerked his head away, got up, casually raised a hand to scratch his large, bulging nose, and went to leave the poker room.

Grant turned a fraction of a second too late. While scanning players at the other two tables, his attention was drawn to the individual walking away, with out-of-place speed. Grant's eyes followed the short, overweight individual who moved smoothly around people without breaking stride. But the face of Eric Clark was hidden from Grant by the angle and by Clark's hand rubbing his nose.

Grant's curiosity was redirected when a very large, imposing figure sat down at his table.

Chapter 10

Jennifer approached two young women at the "Welcome" table – as stated on the sign draped in front of the table – for the "State of Economic Freedom Conference" – as declared on the sign hanging above the table.

"Hello, I'm Jennifer Grant."

"Dr. Grant, welcome! My name is Miranda," chirped a very enthusiastic twenty-year-old with long blond hair, a flawless smile, and lightly tanned skin. "I've got your badge right here."

"Thank you."

The other woman at the table – with a similar smile and equally tanned skin, but long black hair – added, "Here is your packet. I'm Taylor, and I'm thrilled to meet you. I've read lots of your studies and articles, and got very excited when I heard that you not only were speaking at the conference, but that you're an alum. I had no idea."

Jennifer said, "Well, thank you. I was an English major here, and then went on to economics at New York University. Are you both studying economics?"

Taylor answered, "I am. Miranda is a political science major."

"I'm glad to see that you're both interested in the topic of economic freedom."

Taylor said, "Absolutely! I can't wait for your talk on the state of things here in the U.S. Seems to me that we're going in the wrong direction. Anyway, if you need anything for the presentation tomorrow afternoon, or anything else, just let us know."

"I will. But as long as I can access my PowerPoint, I should be all set."

"Great," answered Miranda brightly.

"Hopefully during one of the breaks, we can talk a bit more about your studies."

"Oh, my God, that would be fantastic, Dr. Grant," said Taylor. "You're like a hero of mine. I want to get my PhD in economics as well."

Jennifer smiled. "That's a little scary, Taylor. Not the getting your PhD part, but the hero part. Seriously, though, I'd be glad to talk to you and help out, if I can."

Taylor squealed, and bounced up and down. "Thank you, so much."

Jennifer passed the table, went into the Student Union Ballroom, fixed a cup of tea, and found her way to one of the tables reserved for conference panelists in the front of the room.

Meanwhile, Gil Rice stood on the balcony across from the ballroom. He came inside after Jennifer went into the ballroom. As he approached the "Welcome" table, Miranda asked, "Can I help you?"

"Yes," he replied in a high voice that seemed out of place with a weathered face, thinned hair, and an overweight though hard body. "Do you have a schedule for the conference?"

Miranda said, "Sure." She handed him the conference booklet. "Are you an attendee?"

Rice paged through the program. "Unfortunately, no. I just found out about it."

Taylor volunteered, "You can actually sign up now, if you like."

Rice closed the program. "Thanks, I just might do that." He turned and headed for the stairs.

Chapter 11

Eric Clark pulled his silver Cadillac ATS Sedan into the driveway of the L-shaped ranch-style house he lived in just a few turns off West Sahara Avenue.

No one actually had called him by his given name in a very long time. The few neighbors who spoke to Clark, as well as his coworkers in the city finance department, knew him as Donnie Goodman. This was the life WITSEC had set up for him nearly 18 years ago.

Clark entered the house, and tossed his keys on the kitchen table. After relieving himself in the bathroom, his next stop was a small bar in the living room. He poured two fingers of Scotch, and took a sip.

He looked at the telephone and declared, "Son of a bitch."

Clark grabbed the mobile phone off its cradle, and pushed seven numbers.

When the person on the other end answered, Clark said, "Hey, I've got interesting news."

He listened.

"No, nothing as dull as that. Guess who I almost sat down with at a poker tournament this morning?"

Clark again paused to hear the response.

"Ah, you're no fun. It was Stephen Grant."

Clark smiled wryly while listening this time.

"That's right, Grant."

Clark took another sip of Scotch as the other person spoke. He swallowed and replied, "I was wondering the same, and I was trained long ago not to accept coincidences. It's all about calculations."

The former CIA operative drank again while listening.

"I agree. We need to talk, and figure out what's next."

Chapter 12

The numbers made sense. In fact, it was a no-brainer.

Grant was nearly certain that the very large man, with a shaved head, elaborate goatee, assorted tattoos up and down each arm, and mirrored sunglasses, was about to lose this hand.

Grant actually felt a touch of cockiness. He had not been involved in a truly competitive game of poker in more than 15 years. Yet, here he was as one of the final four players out of the 23 who started several hours earlier.

Two had folded. It was between Grant and the big guy. Once Grant called, each would be all in. The winner would vault to the largest stack of chips at the table, and be guaranteed a share of the tournament prize money. The loser would get nothing, but cold comfort for winding up ahead of 19 other players.

After the flop, the turn and the river, on the table were the two of clubs, two of diamonds, three of clubs, four of spades, and five of hearts. Grant held the five of spades and five of clubs. Odds were that the big guy, sitting diagonally across the table from Grant, had a straight, maybe even seven high. He could have a full house as well. But none of those hands would beat Grant's fives-over-twos full house. Only pocket deuces could snatch the pot from Grant.

After a pause, Grant said, "Call." He pushed his chips forward.

The dealer looked to the big guy, who smiled broadly, with his goatee spreading out rather elaborately. "Sorry, Pastor." He flipped over the two of hearts coupled with a two of spades.

The dealer announced: "Four deuces."

You're kidding me.

Grant didn't bother to turn over his cards. Everyone knew he was done. He merely announced with resignation, "Nice, Rodney."

Grant stood up, and shook hands with each person at the table, wishing them, "Good luck."

Rodney responded, "It was good to meet you, Pastor. And as promised, I'm going to visit St. Matthew's."

"You better," Grant said with a smile, "I'm going to let Pastor Stout know you'll be coming."

Rodney replied, "Hey, I never played poker with a pastor before. Maybe this is a message that I need to get back to church."

As Grant left the Miami Deal poker room, he glanced at his watch. 5:40 PM. Poker was a nice mental exercise and diversion. But sitting at the table for so long, and with Jennifer at the conference, Grant decided physical activity was needed.

A swim, then a walk.

As he headed to the elevators, a voice came from behind. "Pastor Grant."

Stephen turned, and saw Nicky Geraci.

"Nicky, how are you?"

"Good, thanks. Tough break on the tournament."

Grant noted that Nicky's light gray gloves matched his suit. "Ah, you saw that? Well, at least I was competitive."

"You were." Geraci switched topics abruptly. "Dix is in a meeting and has another at seven. He wanted me to invite you to have dinner with him in his suite at Casino Beach."

"What time, and who will be joining us?"

"Eight, and Dix was looking forward to just the two of you."

A little one-on-one time with the father-in-law might not be a bad idea. "Sure, that sounds great."

"Shall I have a car take you over to Casino Beach?"

"No, thanks, Nicky. I was going for a walk later anyway."

Chapter 13

Dix and Stephen sat cattycorner to each other at one end of a long dining room table. This allowed each to look out the large windows at the bright lights of the Strip, and to the less flashy expanse beyond.

The initial talk was casual, focused on the view and Stephen's performance in the tournament, as each man enjoyed a cold Beck's beer.

From the gourmet kitchen came an appetizer of chilled scallop ceviche, with lime, avocado, cilantro, and diced green tomatoes.

Dix picked up his fork, and paused. "Is a prayer in order?"

Stephen replied, "Of course." He folded his hands and bowed his head. Dix followed his lead. "Dear Lord, thank you for all that you've provided, including the opportunity for families to unite. And please bless all of your children who helped prepare the meal from which we are about to partake. We pray this in the precious name of Jesus. Amen."

After chewing and swallowing a bit of the appetizer, Dix said, "I'm glad you and Jenny got together. You're the kind of man I wish she had married the first time around. In my opinion, Jenny saw what she wanted to in Brees. You know, the guy who wanted to make a difference, believed in what she did, blah, blah, blah. I never said anything, obviously, but I saw an opportunist. And believe me, I know opportunists. Ted Brees would become whatever he needed to become. He was a politician in the worst sense of the word. Still is."

Stephen swallowed some of the scallop ceviche. "It's hard to disagree with that assessment today, Dix." Stephen decided to just listen on the subject of Senator Ted Brees. He had his own feelings and thoughts about Jennifer's first husband, and how he mistreated her. Then there were Jen's thoughts about how Ted and Dix were not all that dissimilar in certain respects. In general, though, as Jennifer and Stephen got deeper into their marriage, Ted Brees was growing ever smaller in their rearview mirror.

But Stephen had to ask one question. "Jen cut you off yesterday. What were you going to do to Brees when you heard about his escapades?"

"Well, I could tell you what I wanted to have done to him, to perhaps scare the son of a bitch. But then again, you are a pastor, and probably wouldn't approve. So, I should leave that alone."

Stephen didn't reply as he chewed more of the scallop dish.

The two remained silent through a few additional mouthfuls of food. Then Dix observed, "But then again, with your experience as a SEAL and with the CIA, maybe you would approve, or at least understand."

"Believe me, I understand the impulse." *Leave it at that, Grant.*

"So, if you don't mind me asking, how did you wind up going from the life of a Navy SEAL and CIA agent ...?"

Stephen interrupted, "CIA analyst. My title was 'analyst.'" *Technically true.*

"Right, analyst. So, from the SEALs and CIA to a pastor?"

"It happened over a period of time. I still recognized the importance of the work I was doing, and valued it. In fact, I still do today. But something was gnawing at me, that I should be doing even more. Eventually, I came to realize that I was being called into the ministry."

"Seems like quite a change."

"In terms of day-to-day functions, yes. But at their core, I was and am helping people, just in different ways. Lutherans often talk about being a citizen of two kingdoms – one spiritual and the other earthly. I went from being part of government's earthly role in defending the innocent and dispensing justice, to working for the Lord, if you will, which is about the spiritual, about love, forgiveness, redemption and salvation."

Dix laughed, and shook his head.

Stephen asked, "Something amusing?"

"No, not at all. It's just that such topics don't get much play around here."

"Maybe they need to."

"You're probably right, Pastor." He laughed a bit more.

Dix asked Stephen some basic family questions. Grant relayed how he grew up just outside of Cincinnati, and shared some details about his childhood, from his father's Coca-Cola delivery work to his mother being a librarian, along with his interests in golf, archery, and the Cincinnati Reds.

That last point made Dix laugh, given that Jennifer was such a big St. Louis Cardinals fan. "I guess anything is possible if a Reds fan and a Cards fan can find love."

Stephen continued with the story of how his parents died in a car accident while he was in the Navy. He then skipped quickly over his work with the SEALs, the CIA, and his seminary studies to arrive at becoming the pastor at St. Mary's Lutheran Church.

The empty appetizer plates were removed by the waiter, and replaced by grilled lobster tails with mango dipping sauce.

The conversation bounced around, with Dix inquiring more about Jennifer's work and friends, the Long Island family house, and the recent incidents that Grant had been involved in that had made the news, including serving as a *de facto* bodyguard to a pope and helping to foil terrorists in New York City.

Then it was Stephen's turn to inquire some about his father-in-law. "What about you, Dix? Given that you've worked in Vegas since your teens, you must have had some interesting colleagues, especially in those early years. No?"

"Interesting would be an understatement. For my first twenty years in this business, I learned from the best of what I call pre-corporate Vegas."

Stephen interjected, "You mean, the front men running things for the mob."

Dix smiled and continued smoothly. "Well, that's not exactly how I would put it. I made the transition to corporate Vegas, which is what we still have today, for the most part. Fortunately, I made some very wise investments, took some calculated risks that paid off nicely, and met the right partners. Eventually, we built and ran two successful casinos, and when I sold my shares, I had enough to build Casino Beach, with Nicky and Chet onboard as well."

"Rolled the dice, and came up seven?"

Dix purposefully paused over his lobster tail. "No. There was no rolling of the dice. This was about creating a good business plan, and executing it. Then came The Twenties, and next is The River."

"So, the business end of life has played out nicely."

"I've been fortunate to capitalize on various opportunities."

"What about the rest of life?"

"The rest of life, Pastor? Again, I've been fortunate. No complaints."

Stick your nose in Grant, or not? Why not? After all, he is family. "What about the people in your life?"

Dix wiped the corners of his mouth with a cloth napkin, and placed it back on his lap. "You're thinking about what Jennifer has told you about my relationship with my late wife, with Jenny's mother, Ellen. I never claimed to be perfect, and I regret what I did to Ellen. She deserved better, much better, than what I gave her."

"Dix, while you're my father-in-law, I don't really know you. But as Jennifer's husband, I want to make sure that you realize that when you cheated on Ellen, Jennifer believes that you cheated on her as well."

"She told me that. I tried to explain that it had nothing to do with her. That it was between her mother and me. I was hoping that she would come to see that one day."

"Come on, Dix. You're obviously a smart guy. How can you believe that? Think about how you felt when hearing that Ted cheated on your daughter. Now, what if a grandchild was in the picture? Let's say a little girl. Would you be even angrier with what Ted did, or would you simply accept the declaration that it was just between Ted and Jennifer, and it should not matter to your grandchild?"

Dix's facial expression changed. His smoothness and charm dropped. Grant detected both anger and sadness.

Too far for our first one-on-one?

Dix finished the last of his lobster tail, and got up from the table to look out the window at the lights of Vegas. "You're a bit of a pain in the ass, Pastor."

Grant smiled. "I've heard that, and worse, before."

Dix continued to look out the window, with his back to Stephen.

After a couple of minutes, Stephen got up and walked over to the window. "Listen, I apologize if I crossed a line. You invited me here for dinner. It was not my intention to come across as rude."

After several more seconds, Dix asked, "Why did you tell me that?"

"Two reasons. First, Jennifer is hurting over this. And I don't like it when my wife is being hurt. Second, you and Jennifer still have a chance to rebuild a father-daughter relationship. Like I said, I lost my parents, and I still miss them. I can see the love you have for Jennifer. You need to recognize that you hurt her deeply. Quite simply, Dix, my wife – and your daughter – is right. You didn't just cheat on your late wife, you cheated on your family – Ellen *and* Jennifer. Admit that, talk to Jennifer, and start that process of rebuilding. I can help, or I can keep out of it, whatever is needed or wanted."

Dix didn't look at Stephen. Instead, he continued to stare out the window.

Stephen's BlackBerry rumbled in the pocket of his khaki pants. He saw the time, and thought it would be Jennifer. While Dix still stood silently, Stephen looked at the text message. "Meet me at the Bellagio Fountains in a half hour? Love you."

Stephen broke the silence with Dix. "That was Jennifer. She's apparently finished for tonight at the conference. I'm going to go meet her."

"Yes, of course, Pastor."

"Thanks, Dix. The dinner was excellent."

"You're welcome. I appreciate you coming."

Riding the elevator down, Grant texted, "See you there. Love you as well. By the way, just had dinner with your father."

The quick response: "Oh, great."

Stephen could detect Jen's sarcasm even via text.

Chapter 14

Stephen strolled along the sidewalk, with trees on his left running close to Las Vegas Boulevard South and the Fountains of Bellagio on his right.

The music started, and the fountains came to life.

He spotted Jennifer leaning on a column. The lights and water engulfed her attention.

Stephen quietly approached, catching a glimpse of the water and lights reflected in her brown eyes. He slipped his arms around her waist. "Hello, Dr. Grant."

She clasped her hands behind his neck. "Good evening. Pastor Grant, isn't it? Imagine meeting you here."

They kissed, a little more deeply and longer than they would have on the sidewalk of almost any other road in the country.

Jennifer turned back to the fountains, resting the back of her head on Stephen just below his chin. His hands moved around and met at her stomach.

She sighed. "When you think about a casino in the middle of the desert with a manmade lake and a regular fountain show, it seems silly. But when you're standing here, it really is mesmerizing."

"I agree."

They listened to Frank Sinatra belt out "Fly Me to the Moon" over the many speakers surrounding the waters.

Stephen added, "Apparently there's no getting away from Sinatra on this trip."

Jennifer shrugged. "Hey, it's Las Vegas. This still is Frank's town, right?"

"I think it was Dean Martin who said that it's Frank's world, we just get to live in it."

As Sinatra was concluding, "I love ... you," the fountain waters shot high in the air, and then fell back as the music and lights came to an end.

Jennifer turned and took Stephen's hand. They started walking slowly on the sidewalk, with the many other lights of the Strip darting and leaping. She asked, "So, dinner with my father. How did that go?"

"It went very well, for awhile."

She laughed. "What does that mean?"

Stephen relayed that they caught up a bit on their respective backgrounds, while also mentioning how good the grilled lobster tails were. He concluded, "And we got into his life a bit, and how things were beyond the business aspects. He brought up regrets about how he treated your mom."

Jennifer scoffed, "Regrets, right."

"Then I asked if he realized how he had hurt and cheated on you as well."

Jennifer stopped and looked in Stephen's eyes. "What did he say?"

"He tried to say it was between Ellen and him, and he hoped that you would see it that way one day."

"Same Dixon Shaw."

"Then I told him that he was too smart to actually believe that, and I used an example to drive home the point."

"Really? And..."

"He didn't like it. But I told him that I brought it up because my wife was hurt, and it was clear that he loves you and that he had an opportunity to rebuild some kind of relationship with his daughter, if he just recognized the hurt he caused."

They resumed the walk in silence. Jennifer finally asked, "And what was his response in the end to this son-in-law, father-in-law heart to heart?"

"I left him in somewhat stunned silence, but also in some thought, I think."

They walked a bit more, and arrived outside The Twenties.

Stephen asked, "Are you upset? Should I have let it alone? The conversation just went in that direction, and as I told your father, I don't like it when someone hurts you."

She looked at him, and smiled. "How could I be upset? Thank you for being you. Now, let's go up to our room, make love, and fall asleep."

"I'm really starting to like Las Vegas."

Chapter 15

Gil Rice had prodded and berated the police to find his son. But with nothing developing, the investigation dropped among the cold case files.

Gil, however, was unrelenting.

As time passed, if anyone had been watching, Rice's journey from hope to denial to despair, and finally to anger would have been glaringly apparent. But with his wife dead nearly fifteen years, he had no one else. No one watched because no one cared. As days and weeks went by, he pushed on, trying to figure out what happened to his only child.

More than seven months after Ollie's end, Gil finally, and suddenly, was offered some answers. He could not go to the police, but Rice could act. As a retired prison guard, he often spoke of how the system failed to complete the job of doling out justice. The death of his son would not be one of those instances of failed justice.

Rice could not know what the ultimate intentions were of the mysterious person providing the answers. The individual sounded sympathetic, saying that Ollie's killer had taken a family member of his as well, again with no justice dispensed. This mysterious ally provided aid in Gil's personal pursuit of revenge.

In Chicago, a real estate agent had completed the sale of Rice's home a month earlier. Since he had paid off the mortgage years past, this gave him a chunk of change to carry out his plan.

The purchase of a van and a lease on an old, rundown cattle ranch about an hour northeast of Las Vegas, however, did put a dent in that bankroll.

But his newfound friend promised to help cover the necessary labor, giving Rice backgrounds and contact information on seven individuals who would be assets for this kind of work. Rice selected four. When the job was done, they would disappear.

Rice and his generous friend had the same ultimate objective. But the plan that Rice was now explaining in detail to the four members of his team had a new, extra layer.

The independent contractors didn't object to a little extra work. After all, the added tasks would raise their payday markedly.

Chapter 16

The sanctuary at St. Matthew's Lutheran Church was a half-circle, far wider than it was deep, with high, vaulted ceilings.

The floors were carpeted, and interlocking chairs were thickly cushioned. That boosted the comfort level for worshipers, but tended to muffle instruments and voices in song.

However, since most of the 63 attendees at the two-day "When a Stranger Sojourns: Christian Responses to Immigration" conference were members of the clergy, they sang the hymns during the opening service with a robustness that could not be absorbed by the surrounding fabric.

About half of the attendees were local, but the rest came from varying distances, including California, Arizona, Colorado, New Mexico, Missouri, Indiana, Ohio, Texas, and Illinois. Grant was one of three from the east coast, with the other two from Virginia and Florida.

Since immigration – especially illegal immigration – persisted as a hot topic across much of the nation, this gathering at St. Matthew's earned a far larger response than what the organizers expected.

After the closing hymn, Pastor Jacob Stout returned to the lectern, and reminded everyone that the rest of this day's gathering would be held across an outdoor courtyard in a multipurpose building carrying the name "Luther Family Center."

After getting reacquainted with some colleagues and meeting others for the first time, Grant grabbed a glass of orange juice and some fruit salad, and sat down at one of the ten tables sprinkled around the room in front of an elevated dais. But he immediately got back up when a familiar voice declared, "Stephen, all the way from Long Island. I'm so glad you came."

"Big Jake, it's great to see you."

Stout gave Stephen a big bear hug.

Pastor Jacob Stout – or Big Jake to his close friends – was a classmate with Stephen at seminary. Stout had been a high school teacher and football coach, which was not surprising given a six-foot-three-inch frame that remained strong into his sixties. He also possessed a booming voice and a vigor that likely fit well on the football field.

After retiring from teaching in his mid-forties, he took his wife and kids off to seminary, and wound up with a call to St. Matthew's a dozen years ago.

Stephen continued, "Fortuitous, or kind of freaky, that Jen got the invite to speak at UNLV at the same time as your event."

"Hey, the Lord works in mysterious ways, especially in Las Vegas. And I'm glad He does. How is Jennifer?"

"She's doing well. And what about Zoe, the kids and grand kids?"

"All generally good. We'll talk more, but I've got to introduce our first speaker."

"Go. See you later."

Stephen was looking forward to the first speaker, who would be leading a Bible study on immigration. As a student of history, Grant recognized that the modern climate of opposition, at times overt hostility, to immigration was not new, even though the U.S. was, at the same time, a melting pot. He was hoping to learn more, and be able to take some ideas back to St. Mary's. Given that the debate over immigration periodically got heated on Long Island, he had been pondering a half-day event at St. Mary's. The early plan in his head had Jennifer addressing the economics of immigration, a local professor and friend dealing with the history, and himself undertaking lessons from Scripture and the church.

After introductions and a few amusing remarks, the first speaker said, "Okay, we're going to begin by looking at what Holy Scripture says about how we should treat our neighbors and strangers, as well as the role of governmental authority and laws when it comes to matters like immigration. So, let's start by looking at Leviticus 19..."

Chapter 17

"Jay, please wait until I can come outside. I'll be just a minute." With the baby due any day, Beatrice Aiken was resting at a small kitchen table.

Outside, her husband was placing an extension ladder up against the high ranch that the couple had moved into a few months earlier. "Stay there, Bee. It'll only take a second to change these two floodlights, and then I'm done."

"I'll come out and hold the ladder."

"Nope." He started climbing. "I'm already on it."

Beatrice frowned.

Jay swapped out the first bulb in the two-pronged light, tossing the old bulb onto the grass beyond the concrete patio directly below the ladder. He unscrewed the second, and tossed that down, not far from the first used bulb.

But while pulling the second new bulb from under his arm, Jay moved too quickly. Combined with a light grip, the bulb slipped. Jay lunged to grab the 90-watt halogen that seemed to hang in mid-air for a split second.

Jay missed. The ladder shifted. He lost his balance, and grabbed, in futility, for the home's siding.

"No...!," he called out.

The light shattered on the concrete below, followed by Jay's head.

The ladder clattered to the ground.

Beatrice screamed, "Jay!" She struggled to her feet, and moved as quickly as she could to the backdoor while tears began streaming from her eyes. She prayed aloud, "Please, Jesus, no. Please, no."

* * *

In his very young career as a pastor, Zack Charmichael never had to deal directly with a random death. A death seemingly devoid of meaning. Senseless. That is, until now.

He entered the Aiken home. It was a mere three hours after Jay's body had been taken away. There was quiet sobbing in the distance.

Beatrice's parents – longtime members of St. Mary's – and her two sisters were present.

Her father filled Zack in on some of the details, including that Jay's family, who lived in Oklahoma, had been told. They would be arriving later in the night.

The father told Zack how worried he was about his daughter and the baby, while leading the pastor down a dark hallway to a room with a small light shining.

Beatrice stood looking at her vague reflection in the window, rubbing her protruding stomach as the baby kicked. Her sisters were sitting on the bed. In a nearby chair, Beatrice's mother hid her eyes with her right hand.

In a hushed tone, Zack said, "Beatrice, I'm so sorry."

She turned. Her eyes were red, with deep, dark rings underneath. "Pastor, thank you for coming."

They hugged, and she began weeping again. When she regained her ability to speak, she asked, "Pastor, why would God make this happen? Did we do something wrong?"

"No, Bee, no. God didn't make this happen. I know it's hard. It's a fallen world, and that means death comes. And too often, it's bewildering and harsh. You're struggling with how this could happen to Jay." He looked at the others in the room. "We all are, including me. There are no quick, easy answers. But you're not alone."

One of Beatrice's sisters interrupted, "Nice words, but empty. How can God, any god, exist when things like this happen?"

Zack took a deep breath. "Well, I would say that Jay was not alone in his death. Jesus was with him, and is with him now. Just as He is with us now. That's the comfort, the hope. And as hard as it is right now, I have the confidence that Jay will see us, including his baby, again. We'll be with him in God's kingdom."

Silence fell on the room, but for Beatrice's muffled sniffles. They sat in silence for several minutes.

Zack eventually asked, "Beatrice, would you like to pray?"

She shook her head. "I can't. Not now. I'm too ... too ... angry. Our baby will never know his father. Never."

Zack said, "It's okay to be angry, Beatrice. It really is." Several additional minutes passed. He looked around the room. No one was making eye contact with him. "Beatrice, would you like me to stay, or should I let you, all of you, get some rest, if that's possible?"

"It's okay. Please, go. Thanks for coming."

"I'll be back tomorrow, all right?"

Beatrice nodded.

Zack left more silence behind in the room.

Beatrice's father followed him out. "Is Pastor Grant coming by?"

"He's traveling with Jennifer. I'll call him when I leave here."

At the door, her father said, "Thanks for coming, Pastor Charmichael."

Zack simply nodded in response. The door closed behind him. He got into his Camry, drove to the top of the street, and then pulled over to the side.

He pulled out his smartphone, and called the number at the top of his contacts list. "Hi, Cara."

"Zack, how are they holding up?"

"To be honest, I'm not sure."

Cara added, "How are you holding up?"

"Well..." His voice cracked. "I'm not too sure about that either. I don't think I helped anyone."

"I know that's not true. My dad always says that in horrible times, just being there matters."

"Maybe. Thanks, Cara. I love you."

"You, too."

"I'll touch base later. I have to get back to the church, and call Stephen."

Chapter 18

The assistant dean concluded his introduction of Jennifer Grant by noting, "And as impressive as all of these accomplishments are, I'm most proud to say that she is an alum of our own university. So, without further delay, welcome back, Dr. Grant."

Jennifer walked over in a blue, short-sleeve cotton wrap dress, shook the dean's hand, and took the podium. "Thank you, Dean Bancroft. It's wonderful to be back at UNLV. Since I also grew up in the Vegas area, this very much is a homecoming."

That garnered some applause from the more than 300 in attendance.

"Given that I am an economist today, some might be surprised to hear that while here I majored in English Literature. But that turned out to be a big plus given the amount of writing I do in my economics work. So, thank you to the UNLV English department for making me a better economist today."

She smiled at the additional applause.

"I'd like to take a step a little further back in my Las Vegas educational experience. The first time I really thought about economics was in eighth grade. My teacher was looking at the U.S. as the world's economic leader. She went down a list of things that we were not. So, for example, she mentioned that we did not have the most valued natural resources; we did not have the most farm land; we did not have the most people; and we did not even have the best educational system. That teacher got me wondering. She asked: Why then were we the top dogs in terms of the economy? I waited for the answer. You can imagine how disappointed I was when her response was: I don't know. My teacher basically wrote it off as some kind of mystery."

Jennifer gave a small shake of the head.

She continued, "Interestingly, I didn't get a real answer until I took my lone undergraduate economics class. It was an elective that I didn't take until early in my senior year. But the professor changed my professional direction. He made economics interesting and relevant. Suddenly, I had the tools to explain so much of what happened in business, in politics, and in many other parts of life. And one of his first points was that the difference in economic growth and wealth creation across nations came down to economic freedom. That is, opportunity and prosperity come when individuals are free to start businesses, invest, innovate, invent, create, and work; free to succeed and fail; free to follow their dreams; and free to build and engage in commerce with the confidence that government will establish the rule of law, run a fair system of justice, establish a sound currency, and refrain from imposing heavy tax and regulatory burdens. Despite what my eighth grade teacher and many politicians seem to think, there are few mysteries as to why growth occurs, why economies develop and why wealth is created. It's about economic freedom, that is, it's about the topic that brings us together at this conference."

Jennifer clicked the small remote on the podium to engage her PowerPoint presentation on the large screen hanging on the wall behind her.

"My job this afternoon is to look at the state of economic freedom in the United States. The bottom line: Relative to much of the rest of the world, we look pretty good. Unfortunately, though, we're clearly heading in the wrong direction, and if we continue down this path of less economic freedom, the U.S. economy will suffer accordingly. In fact, we've already seen some significant negatives."

Jennifer clicked the remote to move to the next slide.

"Let's begin by looking at the rule of law, and the protection of life, limb and property..."

Chapter 19

Grant's BlackBerry vibrated on the table in front of him. He appreciated seeing Zack's name. The last panel of the day was becoming noteworthy, unfortunately, for marking a big drop off in the quality of speakers.

He got up, grabbed the phone, and headed for the doors in the back of the room. Once outside, Grant's pace slowed as he hit the late afternoon desert heat.

"Zack, thanks for saving me from an underwhelming panel."

"Stephen, I've got bad news."

"What is it?"

Zack relayed how Jay Aiken had fallen to his death.

Stephen said, "Ah, no. How are Beatrice, and the baby? She's due any day." *Dear Lord, please be with this young family.*

Zack told Stephen about his visit to Beatrice, as well as his doubts about being any help to the family.

"Zack, you make a difference just being there, offering the opportunity for prayer and hopefully providing a ray of hope in the darkness. Tom always makes that point."

"Yes, I know. Cara said the same thing."

"Smart girl you have there." Stephen paused. "It's especially hard when something like this happens, without warning, so random and so young. We have to make sure that we're there – that St. Mary's is there – for Beatrice and the baby."

"Right."

"Okay, I'm going to get back as soon as I can. I need to check with Jennifer to see if she'll stay on until the end of her conference, or come back early with me. Then I'll get a flight, and get back to you with the details."

They went on to briefly discuss some possible, initial logistics for a funeral.

After ending the call, Stephen took a few minutes to walk around on the smooth stones of the courtyard. His eyes rose from the ground to take in the brick exterior of St. Matthews, finally stopping at the cross at the building's peak.

The cross. Death and life wrapped up in one symbol. The brutal, strange and wonderful victory of God incarnate over sin and the death that comes from that sin. 'O, death, where is thy sting?' Well, St. Paul, the sting is there, especially for an expecting mother and her baby. But it's a sting that will heal, eventually giving way one day to heavenly joy. Help us, Lord, to have faith in these grim times. It sure ain't easy.

Grant went back to his phone, and hit Jennifer's number.

Chapter 20

Jennifer asked Taylor and Miranda to join her for the art gallery tour and pre-dinner cocktail party. They jumped at the chance.

Exiting the Student Union, the two students peppered Jennifer with questions about her presentation and career.

Watching from behind, still inside the building, was Gil Rice. He flipped open a cell phone. "Move now. She's in position."

Jennifer's phone played a ringtone – "Makes Me Wonder" by Kenny Chesney – from inside her briefcase. "Ladies, just give me a second to answer this."

Taylor smiled. "I love Kenny Chesney."

Jennifer said, "Me, too." She slipped a strap off her shoulder, and placed the thin briefcase on the sidewalk.

While standing and waiting, Taylor's eyes were drawn to a white van that turned quickly off South Maryland Avenue. Miranda's attention was then grabbed as the vehicle sped toward them.

With her back to the vehicle, Jennifer unzipped a pocket in her attaché, and pulled out the smartphone. It rumbled again, showing Stephen's picture on the screen. "If you'll excuse me for..."

As the van was coming to an abrupt halt just a few feet away, Miranda interrupted, "Dr. Grant, look out!"

As Jennifer turned, the side door of the van slid open and three masked individuals jumped out.

Jennifer, along with Taylor and Miranda, stood frozen, with their mouths agape.

Two of the masked figures descended on Jennifer, while the other pointed a handgun at Taylor and Miranda. The gunman instructed, "Quiet, girls."

Just as Jennifer was about to let out a scream, she was muffled by a gloved hand stuffing a cloth in her mouth. Her attempts to fight back with arms and legs amounted to little against the far bigger and stronger assailants.

Taylor and Miranda still failed to move, with only fright growing on their faces, as Jennifer was roughly taken into the van. The gun remained pointed at the two students as its holder backed into the vehicle.

The door slid closed, and the vehicle quickly moved away.

As the van hit the edge of the parking lot and moved onto the avenue, Miranda and Taylor snapped out of their terror-stricken immobility.

Miranda screamed, "Help! Somebody, please help!"

Taylor called 911.

Jennifer's phone sat on the ground, with Chesney still singing about a couple discovering their love, and Stephen's face still smiling.

Chapter 21

After leaving a message for Jennifer, Stephen went back inside. He opened his MacBook Pro to check flight times back to New York.

* * *

The campus was shut down, and police swarmed over the area.

Witnesses were interviewed on the scene. Three additional people caught at least a glimpse of the abduction. They confirmed the key points passed on by Taylor and Miranda, i.e., a white van, masked men, and the direction the vehicle went after closing its door.

Eventually a member of the police department scrolled through Jennifer's contact list on her phone, and found the ICE entry for Stephen Grant.

He punched the numbers into his own phone.

* * *

Stephen looked at the screen, which declared "Unknown Number." He answered, "Hello?"

"Stephen Grant?"

"Yes, who is this?"

"Mr. Grant, this is Assistant Sheriff Hanson with the Las Vegas Metro Police Department."

Grant's stomach tightened. "Sheriff, is something wrong?"

"Can I ask your relationship to Dr. Jennifer Grant?"

"She's my wife. What's wrong?" The tone in his voice grew more demanding.

"Unfortunately, sir, I have bad news. Dr. Grant has been abducted."

"What!?" *God, please no.* "There must be some mistake."

"Sir, I'm sorry, but there is no mistake."

"What happened? What are you doing to find her? What's the status? Where are you now?"

Grant got brief, unsatisfactory answers from Hanson. He told the sheriff that he would be there shortly.

Abducted? Why? Kidnapped? Why Jen? Dear God, help her. Time to move.

Grant needed a car. He left his belongings behind, and found Pastor Stout seated directly in front of the panelists. "Jake, I need your help. Now."

Jake quickly got up and followed. Stephen explained as he moved to the back of the room. "A sheriff just called. Jennifer's been grabbed."

"Grabbed? What do you mean?"

"She was abducted outside the conference. Masked men in a white van." Grant's mind was swimming. He was working to keep it under control, to get focused. "Can you get me over there?"

"My God, Stephen." Jake stopped, as if trying to process what Grant had told him. "How can that be?"

Grant turned to Pastor Stout. He raised his voice slightly. "Jake, it's happened. You need to get me there now, or just give me a car."

Big Jake's momentary bewilderment gave way to the determination of the old football coach. "Of course. I'll grab my keys, get you there in minutes, and do whatever else is needed." He sprinted across the courtyard to his office.

Within a half-minute, Big Jake's Silverado 1500 bounced out of the church parking lot, briefly screeched on the black roadway, and then sped away.

* * *

The officer escorting Stephen and Big Jake through the police perimeter and to the scene of the abduction called out, "Hanson, this is Mr., ah, I mean, Pastor Grant. Jennifer Grant's husband."

Hanson turned, saying, "Pastor...?"

Grant said, "Yes, that's right. I'm Stephen Grant." He failed to introduce Pastor Stout. "What's the latest, Sheriff?"

Hanson paused for a moment looking at Grant and Stout. The assistant sheriff nearly matched Stout's six-foot-three-inch height, but appeared longer. An elliptical head with thin lips and a pointed nose sat atop his lanky body. The shiny badge on the left side of his chest stood out against his brown shirt. "Pastor Grant, I promise you that we are ..."

"Sheriff, I understand your position, but you can spare the soothing crap, and the baseless promises. Before my pastor days, I was a SEAL and then CIA. I know the realities of situations like this. We need – or you need – to move quickly."

Hanson sighed. "SEAL, CIA, now a pastor – really?" He shook his head. "Anyway, you're right. Moving quickly is what we've done..." He stopped with the buzzing of his phone. "Excuse me." Hanson spoke into the phone, "Plummer, what do you have?" While listening, he grunted and his posture slumped ever so slightly. Eventually, he replied, "Okay, see if there's anything salvageable when they're done."

Grant's anxiety was mounting. "What is it?"

"They switched vehicles, and torched the van on a residential street. And we haven't found anyone who saw the other vehicle or vehicles. These people knew what they were doing."

Son of a bitch.

Hanson continued, "My hope is that this means the abduction was a professional kidnapping, rather than something, well, worse."

"Right." *That's a point.*

"If it's a kidnapping, where would they contact you with demands?"

Grant replied, "We're staying at The Twenties. But there's more. Jennifer is the daughter of Dixon Shaw."

That clearly surprised Hanson. "Shit." He paused. "We've got to get word to Mr. Shaw."

Grant volunteered, "I'll call him."

"Okay. And we need to get set up in your room and in Mr. Shaw's offices."

Grant was on his phone. "Please get me Dixon Shaw. This is his son-in-law, Stephen Grant." While he waited for Dix to come on, Grant was trying to figure out what the next move needed to be. *Where is she? Who did this? It certainly wasn't random.*

Dix said, "Pastor, what can I do for you?"

"Dix, I have bad news…"

Chapter 22

Within a few minutes of each other, a silver sedan and a dark green SUV drove up the long, dusty driveway of the former ranch. They stopped in front of a single story, wood-shingled house with a large porch.

All four of the men working for Rice were fit and muscular. Carlos was short with the sides of his head shaved. Ben stood at a similar height, but with long blond hair and mustache. Dom had narrow eyes, a long nose and black, combed back hair, while Lee was a tall black man who sported a 1970s-like afro.

Dom and Lee carried in a long, black canvas bag, and stopped in front of Gil Rice. He instructed, "In the middle bedroom. Keep her gagged and bound. Today's paper is in there. Take a photo of her with the front-page headline."

Several minutes later, the two men returned. Lee reported, "She ain't going nowhere. And I have the picture." He held up a smartphone.

Rice looked at the picture. "Leave the phone. You two take the first watch by the road. Tell Carlos and Ben to stay on the porch until I call for them."

As he walked down the dirty hallway, any trace of emotion disappeared from Rice's face. He turned the doorknob and entered the bedroom.

Jennifer's arms and legs were bound with zip ties, and duct tape covered her mouth. She was lying on her side on the wood-plank floor.

When she saw Rice's face, the helplessness and fear in her eyes were magnified.

Rice glanced at her, and then looked elsewhere as he paced around the room. He spoke in a hushed tone. "Do you know who Oliver Rice was?"

Jennifer watched him.

Rice shouted, "Did you know Ollie Rice?" He looked at Jennifer, with rage evident.

She shook her head.

Rice turned away from her, and again lowered his voice, as if trying to retain some control. "Of course, you didn't. He was my son. My only family. Dead. Murdered. Lost."

Jennifer's eyes darted around the room.

Rice continued, "Do you know who murdered my son?" He wasn't watching for an answer. "The police don't know. They don't care. It took me months to find out. But I know now. It was your father."

Jennifer shook her head. Tears formed in her eyes. But Rice still was not looking at her.

He raised his voice. "Your father killed my son. Your father, Dixon Shaw!" He turned and moved at Jennifer. His face was distorted, eyes bulging, teeth clenched, veins throbbing, and sweat forming.

Jennifer closed her eyes tight, pushing tears down her skin.

Rice kicked her in the stomach repeatedly. Over and over, he said, "Child for child."

Jennifer managed to roll away and onto her stomach, with her face against the wood floor.

He stopped the attack, and turned away from Jennifer again.

Rice got his breathing under control, and then spoke at one of the dirty walls. "Your father took away my chance.

My chance to make things right with my Ollie. After his mother ... after my wife died, I didn't treat him right. I smacked him around, then I'd feel bad and just leave him alone. I shouldn't have done it. He was just a kid. But I couldn't help it. When I'd finally get her out of my head, I'd look around and there he was. Ollie reminded me of her all the time. I hated him for it. So, I'd push him around some more. That's how it went for a long time, until Ollie finally left. He had the good sense to leave. That's when I finally figured it out. I had to set it right. He wouldn't let me do it. But I knew that I just had to keep at it, every chance I had, to make it better."

He closed his eyes, and clenched his fists. "But then there were no more chances. I had no choice. I had to stop. But once I found out who did it, I knew what I had to do. You were the special bonus to make your father suffer before he dies."

Rice walked over and looked down at Jennifer. "First, you've got to suffer for what your father took from me, and then I'll make sure he suffers."

Tears welled up in Rice's eyes, as he drove his shoe into Jennifer's back several times. "Child for child," he proclaimed again and again.

He went down on one knee, and turned Jennifer over. Her eyes rolled and flittered in pain. Rice screamed, "Child for child!" Jennifer's eyes focused in response. Rice slapped her face several times.

Blood emerged from her nose, mouth and then a gash on her cheek.

Rice finally stopped his attack, and left the room.

Jennifer slipped into unconsciousness.

Chapter 23

Stephen and Dix were back at the dining room table where they had dinner the night before.

But this time, the penthouse was abuzz with police activity. Mobile and hardline telephones were being set up for recording and traces. Calls to the Grants' room would be redirected to Shaw's suite. Email accounts were open on large computer screens.

Grant fought to maintain his focus. He tried to tap his SEAL and CIA training, looking to push back the emotions so that he could think and act clearly. But for all of the critical assignments at various points on the globe, and for all the parishioners he helped in times of crisis, nothing compared to this. Jennifer had been taken.

Grant didn't know where she was, or what was happening to her. He had no clue who did this. He struggled to fight off images of her being abused, and then what he would do to the perpetrator, or perpetrators, if that turned out to be the case.

All Grant knew was that when he figured this out, that person, or those people, would regret their actions.

Some would advise that he ask God to forgive what he was now longing to do. But that was not in him at the moment.

Dix and Stephen stared across the table at each other, as activity buzzed around them.

Dix said, "Is this all we can do, just fucking sit here and wait?"

Grant knew that his father-in-law was not a man built for waiting. In that sense, at least, they were alike.

Sheriff Hanson also was seated at the table. While Shaw's question was rhetorical, an expression of anger, Hanson nonetheless responded. "Our people are combing the area. Everything from the crime scene is being examined..."

Dix waved his hand in the air, interrupting, "Yes, yes, of course."

Hanson refocused. He looked at Grant and then Shaw. "Mr. Shaw, Pastor Grant, is there anyone you can think of who might be behind this? Does Jennifer have any enemies?"

Shaw replied incredulously, "Enemies? She's an economist."

Grant looked at Dix. *Any enemy is more likely to be focused on you or me, Dix. From my CIA days, or your business dealings. No doubt, we both dealt with some unsavory types, at least years ago. Of course, in the end, it's probably about money.*

Grant said, "Sheriff, she's no doubt pissed some people off over the years with her writings and testimony on all kinds of issues. But that's unlikely to result in a kidnapping. Don't you think it's probably about money, given the family's wealth?"

Hanson replied, "I expect a financial demand, Pastor Grant, but there's often some kind of personal connection as well, somewhere along the line, an additional motivation."

True.

"That additional motivation, as you put it, could be tied to either of us." Grant pointed to Dix and himself.

"Right." Hanson nodded. "Those were going to be my next questions. Can you, Mr. Shaw, and you, Pastor Grant, think of anyone that you've crossed paths with that would want to hurt you and your family? I wouldn't normally ask that of a pastor, but you did say that you used to be with the CIA, right?"

"Yes, I did...," Grant began, but Dix interrupted him.

"You've got to be kidding, Hanson. I've been in the casino business for nearly a half-century. This is a tough business. Sometimes people – a good number of people – lose. They take a big hit, and they're not happy about it. You want a damn list of people that I may have angered over the years?"

Hanson replied evenly, "Yes, I do. Pick the ones that stand out, and the last time you saw them."

Dix shook his head, and then waved over Nicky Two Gloves, who was standing watch over the room with his back to the large windows overlooking Vegas. Shaw announced, "Let's make a list of the people that I've pissed off over the years, Nicky. The ones that really hate me."

Hanson turned to Grant. "What about you, Pastor? Anyone from your former line of work that we should look at?"

Problem is that there are too many? And they're global and closely tied to political power. At least, the ones still alive. "Let me think about that, Sheriff." Grant knew the person he had to contact. He told Hanson, "I'm going to make a call."

Chapter 24

Paige Caldwell casually swam in the warm waters, while keeping an eye on the Iranian Quds Force officer sitting poolside.

The Iranian's dark, olive skin blended into the night. But the dim lighting around the pool highlighted his large eyes, and white shirt and pants. Given the man's girth, he looked like a Middle Eastern version of the Stay Puft Marshmallow Man.

Caldwell smiled at a muscular, fair-skinned man, with blond hair that had been reduced to a crew cut, sitting several tables away from the Iranian. Sean McEnany was one of Caldwell's partners in a firm that worked as a private contractor for the CIA, and others. He appeared relaxed in a tan polo shirt, khaki shorts and brown sandals, sipping on a beer and watching Paige. They seemed to be a couple on vacation.

The only others in the area were a young couple intertwined at the far end of the pool, and a gray-haired couple stretched out on chaise lounges. Their eyes were closed, and their joined hands hung between the two lounges.

A waiter occasionally appeared to see who needed drinks refreshed.

The resort took up all of a tiny island in the Dominican Republic. The pool sat just 80 yards away from one of the island's docks that jetted into a large lagoon. The lagoon in turn emptied into the Caribbean.

The Iranian waited.

Paige and Sean waited. Their intelligence said that the target would be meeting the Iranian this night at this exact location.

The information turned out to be entirely accurate.

A thin, average-height man with thick black hair, and matching eye brows, approached the Iranian's table. They shook hands, and sat down. A waiter quickly appeared. They ordered. The waiter disappeared.

Caldwell gave a tilt of the head to McEnany.

She swam toward the two men, and looked directly at the Iranian. His eyes locked on Paige as she rose out of the waters, squeezing water from her long black hair and showing off a fit, freckled body in a tiny, white, strapless bikini. The Israeli, who had just sat down with the intention of trading a cache of Mossad secrets for a very large payday, turned to see what his Iranian contact was eyeing. Paige Caldwell seized his attention as well.

She smiled provocatively, and said, "What are you two handsome gentlemen up to on such a beautiful night?"

The Israeli traitor began, "Well, my dear..."

But he was interrupted by the low, raspy voice of Sean McEnany, who had moved in from the opposite direction. It was no surprise that McEnany went unnoticed compared to Caldwell. He said, "Isn't it obvious? They're transacting secret business."

The Israeli and Iranian whirled their heads around at the sound of his voice. But before they got a look at his face, they stopped at the Glock G30S, with a suppressor attached, in McEnany's hand.

While the Iranian gave a look of resignation, the Israeli initially panicked. He slid his chair back. But before he could get fully to his feet, Caldwell struck like a cobra. She had her arm tightly around his neck in a second, and whispered in his ear, "You have two choices. We leave you dead poolside, or you quietly come with us. Which is it?"

He relinquished. "I get it."

McEnany said, "Smart choice." He pointed the gun at the pathway leading away from the pool and the resort buildings. "That way."

The two men got up and started to move.

Caldwell looked around. One couple was still in the throes of passion in the pool. The other still held hands, but the man's eyes were now open, squinting in their general direction. Caldwell spotted the waiter returning with two drinks on a tray. She told McEnany, "Signal Charlie, and get them down to the dock. I'm right behind you."

She sat down at the table, as the waiter arrived. He looked a bit bewildered, as he watched the three men move away.

Caldwell said, "Thank you, so much. You can leave the drinks. My friends will be back in a bit." She smiled at him.

"Yes, of course, señorita. Do you need anything else?"

"A piña colada would be heavenly."

The waiter scampered off.

Paige looked at the drinks on the table. She took a long drink of the Cuba Libre through a straw, and said to herself, "Needs more lime."

Paige rose from the table, and caught the gray-haired man staring at her. He was smiling. She smiled back, shook her finger at him, turned, and went down the path to the dock.

As she stepped on the wood planks, the nondescript white fishing boat piloted by Charlie Driessen, the third partner in the firm, smoothly approached. McEnany directed his two captives onto the boat, giving the unsure Iranian a shove, which resulted in the Quds Force operative landing face down on the deck. After McEnany, Paige stepped onboard.

With his unruly, gray mustache and sparse hair, Driessen played the part of the weathered fisherman well. As he throttled the boat forward, he looked at Paige and said, "Traveling light tonight? I don't see where you could possibly hide a weapon."

"I have to leave something to your imagination, dirty old man."

"Hey, I'm far from being that old, and you're not leaving much to imagine."

"Just the best parts."

Driessen laughed.

McEnany kept the gun trained on their guests.

The nervous Israeli asked, "Who are you? CIA?"

McEnany replied, "Not exactly. But have no fear, you'll be with our CIA colleagues soon."

Caldwell added, "It's rather a shame that the CIA will not be the end of your journeys though. It's just a stopover. In the end, both of you gentlemen will wind up in the very capable hands of Mossad. Of course, our Israeli friends are rather grumpy. I would not want to be either one of you."

A smartphone on a tray next to Driessen lit up and buzzed. He glanced down, and read the name on the screen. Driessen held up the phone. "Hey, Paige, guess who?"

Paige looked to both Charlie and Sean. "It's Stephen. He'd only call this number in an emergency."

Charlie grunted, while Sean nodded.

She answered, "Stephen, while it's always great to hear from you, can I get back later? Kind of busy, right now."

On the other end of the call, Grant announced, "I'm sorry, Paige, but I need your help, immediately. It's a matter of life and death – Jennifer's life."

"What happened?"

As the boat glided smoothly across the dark waters of the Caribbean, Paige listened as her one-time partner, and former lover, relayed that his wife had been kidnapped. Stephen needed Paige to see if anyone from his CIA days could be tracked to Las Vegas, or if any of them had newly popped up on radar in troubling fashion.

Paige replied, "Stephen, on our way to drop off two packages, and then we're on it."

"We?"

"Charlie and Sean are with me."

During his CIA days, Stephen had worked with Charlie Driessen as well. Recently, under difficult circumstances, Paige and Charlie left the CIA to become contractors. The CIA put them together with McEnany, a former Army Ranger and an officer at a corporate and government security firm with deep contacts running inside and outside government. The depth of his contacts remained a mystery even to his partners, Caldwell and Driessen.

McEnany also happened to be a member of Grant's parish for the past few years, including as leader of the evangelism committee on church council. He had aided Grant with some unique, non-clergy challenges, and then began working with Paige and Charlie per the CIA's recommendation. Grant's curiosity about Sean's work and background had grown, including some questions creeping into Grant's mind as to how and why Sean wound up at St. Mary's.

Stephen replied, "Good. I need all of you."

Paige declared, "You've got us."

Chapter 25

After the Iranian and Israeli were deposited with an appreciative CIA team, Caldwell, Driessen and McEnany quickly returned to the small house they were operating from in Santo Domingo.

Driessen pulled the dark blue Range Rover into the open-air carport. The three climbed the stairs up to the main floor of the house.

Paige said, "I'm contacting Noack at FBI to make sure he knows what's going on."

McEnany chimed in, "I'll start poking around for any links to Stephen's background. But first, I don't know if anyone has contacted our church. I'm going to call St. Mary's, and my wife."

Charlie added, "I'll get the coffee going. An already long day and night promises to get a hell of a lot longer."

McEnany moved into one of the small bedrooms to make his call, as Paige sat down at the kitchen table. While punching keys on her encrypted phone, she said to Charlie in a low voice, "He's calling their church? I've never really gotten it, with both Sean and Stephen, especially in this line of work."

As he scooped coffee grounds into a filter, Charlie grunted, "You don't have to understand it, Paige. Maybe they just need it."

Nearly 1,500 miles away, after one transfer, Special Agent Rich Noack picked up the phone on his crowded desk. "Noack."

In recent years, during a variety of events and challenges, Noack had come to know Stephen Grant, Paige Caldwell, her team, and their abilities. He also made clear that he appreciated what they had done in service of the nation.

"Rich, it's Paige Caldwell."

Noack eased his weighty, six-foot-six-inch frame back in the chair, and rubbed his bald scalp. "Paige, my favorite ex-CIA operative. You caught me working late. To what do I owe the pleasure of this call?"

His lightness of attitude gave way to a grim focus as Paige explained what was going on in Las Vegas.

Noack concluded their conversation, "Okay, I'm not messing around with this. I'll contact our Las Vegas field office, get an update, and let them know that Nguyen and I are on our way. We should have wheels down in seven hours or so." He glanced at his watch. "About two-thirty or three local."

"Thanks, Rich."

After ending the call, Paige said to Charlie, "We need to get to Vegas. Now."

Sean had re-entered the room. "I'm going to stay here." He pointed to the extensive computer and communications system set up in the living room. "We've got everything here for me to get at the right people and information, and not waste time traveling. You two go."

Chapter 26

For a few minutes, Pastor Zack Charmichael sat quietly on the couch in his living room after hanging up with Sean McEnany.

He finally stirred, shut off the television and xBox 360, and walked down the short hallway to his bedroom. Zack lowered his knees onto the padded beam of a Maplewood kneeler, pulled out a small devotional based on Martin Luther's writings from a lower shelf, and opened the book where he would normally rest his folded hands. He flipped pages until he found what he wanted.

Zack looked at the crucifix hanging just a few feet away on the wall. He blessed himself, looked down, and read aloud from *Through Faith Alone*:

> But in the middle of trials and conflicts, it's difficult to call out to God, and it takes a lot of effort to cling to God's Word. At those times, we cannot perceive Christ. We do not see him. Our heart doesn't feel his presence and his help during the attack. Christ appears to be angry with us and to have left us. Then during the attack, we feel the power of sin, the weakness of our bodies, and our doubt. We experience the flaming arrows of the devil and terrors of death. We feel the wrath and judgment of God. All this

raises very powerful and horrible shouts against us so that there does not appear to be anything left but despair and eternal death. However, in the middle of these terrors of the law, the thundering of sin, the shaking of death, and the roar of the devil, the Holy Spirit in our hearts begins to call out, 'Abba! Father!' And his cry is much stronger and drowns out the powerful and horrible shouts of the law, sin, death, and the devil. It penetrates through the clouds and heaven and reaches up to the ears of God.

Zack raised his head, and looked at the crucifix. "Please, dear Lord, be with Jennifer. Protect her, and give her strength."

He rose from the kneeler, went back over to his bed, and sat down with slumped shoulders. He flipped through the contacts on his iPhone until he found Tom Stone. As the phone rang, Zack closed his eyes and rubbed his forehead.

Father Tom Stone answered, "Zack? Need some nighttime gaming advice?"

"Tom, I just got a call from Sean McEnany."

"What's wrong?"

"Jennifer has been taken, kidnapped out in Vegas."

"What? No way. You must be wrong."

After Zack repeated the basic message, Tom said, "God, please no." He took a deep breath. "Tell me the rest of what you know."

Zack passed on what Sean had told him. He finished, "Unfortunately, that's all I know."

Tom's voice revealed frustration and anger. "I can't believe this. All right, have you touched base with anyone else?"

"Not yet."

"I'll get a hold of Ron, and Joan and George. You take care of St. Mary's. Does that make sense?"

"Yes, will do."

"And Zack, make sure you let me know when you hear anything."

"Absolutely, and please do the same."

"Of course. And pray."

"Already doing so."

Chapter 27

It was just a few minutes after 10:00 PM in Las Vegas when the phone rang. For the briefest moment, everyone in the room froze.

The call was coming in on the line to which Grant's room was being forwarded.

Grant fought to control the impulse to immediately grab it. *They're calling me.* He looked at Sheriff Hanson to make sure they were ready.

Hanson nodded.

Grant picked up the phone. "Yes."

"This is Pastor Stephen Grant?"

"Yes."

"I'm calling about your wife, Jennifer."

Grant struggled to control his anger. "I swear if you harm her in any way, I will kill you."

"Now, that doesn't sound like a pastor," observed Gil Rice on the other end of the call.

"I've been many things in my life besides a pastor."

"Yeah, okay. Tell your father-in-law that he needs to get his hands on $15 million. Bearer bonds with coupons attached. Those are supposed to be kind of hard to come by these days, but I know that the rich, connected Dixon Shaw will make it happen."

He spit out Dix's name.

Grant started to reply, "But that might..."

"No buts, Pastor Grant. Make it happen. I'll call back at noon tomorrow with instructions."

"Wait, damn it. Nothing's going to happen until I know that Jennifer is all right. I need to speak with her."

"That's not really an option. But don't worry. Check Shaw's email. You'll see that your wife is okay."

The call ended.

Grant looked at Hanson, and demanded, "What did you get?"

Hanson checked with his team, and shook his head. "Nothing."

Grant clenched his teeth. *Sean better have something.*

Shaw yelled, "What do you mean nothing? What fucking good are you people?"

An officer sitting at one of the computer screens announced, "Mr. Shaw, an email with no subject line but an attachment just came into your account."

Shaw and Grant came over to look at the screen. Dix ordered, "Open it."

And there was Jennifer, mouth gagged, hands behind her back, leaning up against a dirty, white wall with today's newspaper resting below her chin.

Dix said, "Jenny, oh, Jenny."

Grant stared at her eyes. *Photo means nothing. Could have been anytime today. She could be... Don't go there. She's so scared. All of my training and experience, and I'm sitting here helpless. Wait until noon tomorrow? No way. Who is this bastard? Got to make something happen. I've got to get to her. Lord, I desperately need your help.*

Hanson looked at Dix. "Mr. Shaw, can you get $15 million in bearer bonds by noon, in case we need them?"

Dix replied, "We don't have my daughter, Sheriff Hanson, but I do have the funds. That's not an issue." His voice was drenched in frustration. "Can your team perhaps track the email, and figure out who has taken Jennifer and where she is?"

* * *

Rice entered the room.

Jennifer's right eye was swollen shut, but she was awake.

Rice walked over, and looked down at her lying on the floor.

"Your husband, a fucking pastor, threatened to kill me." He laughed and shook his head. "I'm not the one who's going to die. Your father will hand over money. He will know that he lost his only daughter. And then he will die."

Rice grabbed a clump of auburn hair with his left hand, and pulled Jennifer up. Her body hung, with her buttocks barely touching the floor. With bound hands and legs, she was unable to gain any balance or grab onto something to relieve the pain.

"I will never see Ollie again, and Dixon Shaw will never see you again. Child for child." No slap to the face this time. He clenched his right hand into a tight fist, and drove it into the left side of her face.

With the force and momentum of his own blow, Rice dropped Jennifer to the floor.

Chapter 28

After the ransom call, Hanson and his Las Vegas Metro Police team extended their operations farther across the dining and living rooms of Shaw's penthouse suite at Casino Beach. They coordinated officers in the field, and tapped into the FBI.

Stephen was in near-perpetual motion. He moved amidst the police, then to his own laptop that had been brought over from Big Jake's church, and back again with Hanson's people. He repeatedly looked at his BlackBerry, waiting for Paige or Sean to come through with something … anything.

Grant needed information to act, but didn't have it. He also needed to focus, but failed at that as well. *Lord, she doesn't deserve this. Help me find her.*

Dix, meanwhile, announced that he had to work on getting the bearer bonds, and went into his office behind a closed door with Nicky Geraci and the newly arrived Chet Easton.

After instructing Chet to have the bonds ready, Dix asked his two partners, "Who the hell is doing this?"

Nicky replied, "It could be anybody on that list we gave Hanson."

Dix shook his head. "But none of those characters really feel right to me on something this extreme, this crazy. Shit, there are a lot of ways to screw me over if you didn't like how our dealings turned out that don't risk getting nailed for kidnapping, and God only knows for what else. No, this person is unhinged. Nuts."

Nicky stared down at his hands while adjusting his thin, brown gloves. He shrugged, "Not necessarily, Dix. It could just be about a big payday. Or, your son-in-law could be the reason. It's clear from what we've dug up that he wasn't just an analyst for the CIA. The guy likely made enemies."

"I know. But why here in Vegas then? Why now?"

Chet pushed his glasses up and answered, "Think about it. You have the money, and Grant gets hit where it hurts most."

Shaw's eyes bore in on Easton. "Where Grant gets hurt most, Chet? She's my daughter. She's where I get hurt most."

"Of course, Dix. I did not mean otherwise."

Dixon Shaw's calm, cool charm was gone. He slammed his hand down on the glass-top desk, and hissed, "This is our fucking town. Two Gloves, get our people moving."

"I've already got them on it, Dix. They're turning the area inside out."

"Squeeze everyone. I want my daughter found. I want the son of a bitch we heard on that call dead. Do you both read me? Dead."

Chapter 29

The encrypted cellphone vibrated. Gil Rice answered, "Yes."

The caller declared, "This was not the plan."

"Another layer to the plan, but the end result will not change."

"That's what you say, but reaching that goal has become tougher."

"I disagree. We both want the same thing, right? The death of Dixon Shaw," said Rice.

"Yeah, but..."

"No, no buts. This is better than just killing Shaw. First, his money. Then we take his daughter, just as he took my son and your loved one. And then, he loses his life. I don't see how this could be any better."

"Yes, I understand that. But her husband..."

Rice chuckled. "Who? The pastor?"

The caller added intensity to his voice. "You don't understand. He's no ordinary pastor. He has a unique background. He was a Navy SEAL and then CIA."

"Really?" A trace of surprise leaked into Rice's response.

"And he's not the type to forgive, and rest after his wife dies."

Rice sighed. "You're right. He won't. Just like you and I haven't."

"Well, what are you going to do?"

"The only thing that can be done. You got me good guys on this team, right?"

"Of course," replied the caller.

"Then I'll up their pay, and we'll put another item on the to-do list. Pastor Grant will have to die as well."

"That's fine. Make it clean. Leave nothing for anyone to track back."

"You don't have to remind me," said Rice.

Chapter 30

It was nearly 3:30 in the morning, and Grant had not even thought about shutting his eyes.

Nor did he have to rely on coffee to stay awake, as was the case with everyone else in the suite. He had sipped water, and taken bites of fruit over the past few hours.

The ringing of a phone set the room into action. It was Stephen's BlackBerry. He looked at the screen, and announced, "Not the kidnappers."

Stephen said, "Hello, Paige."

Caldwell asked, "Have you heard anything?"

"No. He's supposed to call at noon, and the local police have got nothing." Anger emanated from Grant's voice, something that his old partner would not miss.

"Charlie and I are downstairs."

"How the hell did you get here so fast?"

"It's amazing what can be done with a private jet. Listen, you need a break. Meet us near the main doors. Now."

She's got something important, and isn't sure who should know. Grant upped his voice a hair. "Yeah, you're right, I need to walk around. I'll be down in a few minutes."

Grant ended the call. He looked at Dix and Hanson. "The old friends I called earlier are here. They might be able to help when this breaks. I'm going to meet them downstairs. Join the ranks of coffee drinkers perhaps. I need something."

Shaw nodded.

Grant looked at Hanson. "I'll be back up in a little while, but call me, obviously, if anything happens." He held up his phone to further make the point.

Hanson said, "Of course. Go clear your head, Pastor Grant."

On the elevator ride down, Grant was trying not to get his hopes up that Paige and Charlie had something solid to act on. He struggled to stop running grim scenarios through his head as to how this all might play out. He tried to focus on finding Jennifer, hugging her and never wanting to let her go.

When the elevator doors opened, Grant practically jumped forward. He moved quickly around a couple of turns, and past a casino floor that still buzzed with activity at this wee hour of the morning.

As he spotted Paige and Charlie lingering off to the side of the front entrance, a calm confidence began to build inside Stephen, working against the fear.

Stephen hugged Paige, letting her speak.

"Stephen, I'm so sorry this happened. But we're going to get her back."

The fear pushed back against the calm. He replied in a low voice. "Thanks, Paige, for coming. I hope you're right."

Charlie shook hands with Stephen. He whispered, "Shit, Grant, you know Paige doesn't say anything without good reason. We've got a potential location."

Grant grabbed on tighter to the calm. "What do you have?"

Paige said, "Sean came through. It looks very good. Come on, we'll explain on the way. We've got a car out front. I made it worthwhile for the valet to keep it ready."

Grant replied, "How far?"

Charlie said, "Little over an hour north."

"Lay out?"

"According to McEnany, an old ranch."

Grant started running options through his head. Time. Darkness. He decided. "Let's go. We need to make this happen before sunrise."

"Agreed," said Paige.

"We'll make a quick, five-minute stop," added Charlie. "A friend can equip us as needed."

Calm and confidence was taking over. Grant said, "Good."

They moved through the front doors into the dry night air, and ran right into the large frame of FBI Special Agent Rich Noack, accompanied by Special Agents Trent Nguyen and Jessica West.

Caldwell, Driessen and Grant knew Nguyen, but West was new to the mix.

Noack said, "Where the hell are the three of you going?"

Grant responded, "Good to see you, Agent Noack. We're going to get my wife. We could use your help."

"That's why we're here."

Charlie interrupted, "Good. Information on the way. No time to delay. We've got to make a quick stop to get armed properly, and then..."

"No need for that," said Agent West. She stopped and looked at Noack, who nodded his approval. She continued, "Our vehicle is stocked with everything we need."

Paige said, "I'll ride with our FBI friends to bring them up to speed. We'll follow Charlie. Stephen go with Charlie, and he'll fill you in. Don't call the group upstairs until you know everything."

What does that mean?

Chapter 31

Driessen maneuvered the rented, silver Chevy Equinox away from the Strip and onto Interstate 15, with West at the wheel of the dark Chevy Suburban following close behind.

Once on the freeway and accelerating, Charlie glanced at Grant in the passenger seat, and started to explain. "McEnany's not exactly transparent as to how he gets information like this. He does this mysterious shit all the time. His information is always on target, but since I work with the guy, I'd like something more as to where he gets this stuff."

Grant interrupted to get Driessen focused. "Charlie."

"Yeah, right. Anyway, he apparently managed to get somebody over at NSA to move on this. The encryption on the kidnapper's call was heavy, asymmetrical. Couldn't get where it started. But on the follow-up email, they let their guard down apparently. Weaker, symmetrical encryption. While we were in the air, McEnany, and whoever the hell is helping him, cracked it and pinpointed the general location from where it was sent. A little more digging, apparently some Google Maps and online real estate listings, and we seem to have them holed up on an old ranch not far from Mesquite. Also, once they found where the email came from, they went back and deciphered that the kidnapping call came from the same place. So, as long as they haven't moved, we seem to be on target."

Stephen said, "Thank God for Sean and his mysterious contacts, transparent or not."

"Amen to that, I guess."

"But why did Paige say to hold off letting the group back at the hotel know all of this?"

"Well, it gets dicey. The NSA guy was able to poke around more intelligently now. Not long after the kidnapping call, an encrypted call was picked up starting from the Strip area, while the same level of encryption came in at the ranch area."

Grant blurted out, "Son of a bitch. You mean someone in the hotel called the kidnappers?"

"Well, at least somewhere in the general area."

Paige Caldwell relayed the same information to Noack and his team in the Suburban.

No one from either vehicle called the suite at Casino Beach. However, Noack did call the Las Vegas FBI field office for additional assistance.

Chapter 32

Driessen exited Interstate 15, and after making a quick left and traveling a couple of miles, he pulled off to the side of the road. They were about a quarter of a mile from the ranch.

The six met at the rear of the Suburban. Agent West opened the back doors.

West was slim and nearly as tall as Grant, with long blond hair, pulled up in bun, and bright blue eyes. She pointed to the equipment, announcing, "Vests. Radio earpieces. Hand guns. Hope you're okay with Glocks."

"Our weapon of choice," answered Caldwell.

West handed out weapons and ammunition to Caldwell and Driessen. But she hesitated when turning to Grant. She looked at his neck.

Grant had forgotten that he started yesterday at Big Jake's conference in his clergy collar, and it never occurred to him to change. He pulled the white strip from the collar of the black shirt, and snapped open the two top buttons. He asked, "That better, Agent West?"

West was a bit startled. "Oh, of course. I didn't mean anything."

"Got a Glock 20?"

She found and handed him the gun, with several 10-round magazines.

Grant looked at the weapon. "That'll work just fine."

The three FBI agents – Noack, Nguyen and West – removed their dark suit jackets to slip on the bulletproof vests. Caldwell, Driessen and Grant followed the FBI team's lead with the vests. Radios were checked.

Caldwell asked, "Tactical knives?"

West replied, "Do you think that's necessary?"

Trent Nguyen, who had been largely silent since touching down in Las Vegas, interjected, "Since we don't know what we're up against, yes, better to have options."

The 40-year-old Nguyen was approaching legend stature in the FBI. He was highly decorated, professional, smart, and well-liked. He excelled in the field, and shunned any promotion that would mean more time behind a desk. For good measure, Nguyen, who was born in Saigon to an American nurse and a Vietnamese businessman, was never shy about sharing his love for the U.S. In recent months, Noack had started calling him Captain America.

Nguyen continued, "We know four were involved in grabbing your wife, Pastor Grant. But we don't know how many people are on this site."

Noack said, "Correct. That unknown is why we're going to wait for the backup I called in."

Paige shot a look at Stephen.

Grant declared, "We're not waiting for anyone else. We have to move immediately."

"Now wait a second...," Noack started to reply.

"Listen, Noack, first, we have no idea what's happening to my wife. Second, this is an open location. Our only chance is to move in under the cover of darkness. And we have less than an hour of darkness left. Waiting for your backup means increasing the chances that Jennifer will die."

Noack sighed, and looked at Nguyen. "Trent?"

Nguyen said, "He's right, Rich. We don't know how many are in there, but if we wait..."

Caldwell added, "There's no real choice."

Noack acquiesced. "I don't like it. But you're right. Okay, West pull up the satellite view of the place on that tablet."

Their improvised, stealth assault on the ranch was sketched out quickly.

As they moved, Grant prayed silently for God's help, while pushing aside the impulse to also request forgiveness for what he was thinking of doing to Jennifer's kidnappers.

Chapter 33

Noack, Nguyen and West went along the side of the road, moving closer to the ranch entrance, while Caldwell, Driessen and Grant made a loop through uneven terrain in order to approach the small house from a different direction.

The three FBI special agents were spread out by several yards. Nguyen whispered into his microphone, "We've got two males leaning against an SUV."

"See 'em," answered Noack.

"They're pretty open," assessed West. "Options?"

"Here's how it's going to happen," commanded Noack. "You two will quietly move to positions behind the SUV. I will get around in front of them, staying out of their sight. Looks like there's some cover behind those bushes along the fence. Once you're in position, signal me. I'll get their attention, and then you're going use those tactical knives that West didn't think we'd need to save my ass without firing a shot. Got it?"

"Risky, Rich," volunteered Nguyen.

"Can't afford the noise of a firefight with the hostage. Besides, how risky can it be when you have Captain America on your team?"

West said, "Captain who?"

Nguyen declared, "Never mind."

"There's one weakness," said West. "It's obvious that you two should get behind them, while I approach."

Noack replied, "Negative. Why?"

"I have certain assets that will restrain their impulses to shoot, at least initially. Trust me."

Noack looked over at West. She was taking off her vest. Then she opened the top three buttons on her light blue shirt, and unraveled her long blond hair.

Nguyen observed, "Makes sense, Rich."

Noack replied, "Okay, but I'm getting a little tired of being second-guessed."

Nguyen said, "Don't worry. You're still our fearless leader, like Nick Fury."

Noack continued, "Jessica, be careful, and wait for our signal that we're in position."

"Naturally," she answered.

The two men moved off to the left, and crossed the small road. Nguyen moved with greater ease than did Noack, who in fact spent far more time at a desk and in conference rooms than in the field or the gym. That took a quicker toll on his fitness as he approached fifty. But Noack kept up, and maintained stealth.

West crept further along the road, and settled in behind the small bush and porous fence. There was no indication that the two men – Dom and Lee – had seen or heard anything. West looked down at the ground, grabbed some dirt and rubbed it on her shirt, neck and one cheek. She shook her hair to make it more disheveled.

Nguyen and Noack were in position. Nguyen was positioned behind Lee and his afro, while Noack took an angle on Dom.

Noack whispered into his mouthpiece, "West, we're good."

Jessica West took a deep breath, rose, and started walking with a limp and a bit of a stagger. She had crossed the road before the two guards spotted her. They moved from leaning on the vehicle to standing upright. Their guns – AK47s – were shifted into ready positions. Each man took a step forward.

West waved. "You guys, hey, can you help me?" She sounded drunk. "My car went off the road up there." She motioned in exaggerated fashion, indicating where her fictional car was. She laughed. "I kinda drank too much."

Dom said, "What do we have here?" He smiled broadly.

Lee whispered, "Careful."

Dom replied, "Of what, this girl? I think our night just got a lot more interesting, Lee."

Lee called, "Are you alone, ma'am?"

West staggered a bit once more. "Unfortunately. Can you please help? Oh, you have guns. Are you police?"

Dom whispered, "Like I said, a lot more interesting."

As Dom swung his weapon over his shoulder with the attached strap, Nguyen moved first. With knife in hand, he swept in on Lee. Though several inches taller and certainly having larger muscles than Nguyen, Lee had no chance. Nguyen had surprise and the advantage of the first move. Those two facts made the outcome for Lee inevitable. Trent Nguyen was a perfectionist. The knife entered through Lee's back. Nguyen made sure it went deep. Lee dropped to his knees, lingered there for a second, and then fell forward.

At the same time, Dom had spotted Nguyen just as he arrived behind Lee. As Dom struggled to pull his weapon back off his shoulder, Noack arrived like a massive nose tackle. Noack wrapped his left arm around the kidnapper, and as the two descended toward the ground, the FBI special agent maneuvered the knife's position in his right hand. As the weight of the two men hit the hard ground, the knife drove through Dom's flesh, bone, and lung.

Noack rolled off the man, and ripped his knife out while doing so.

West had her gun out scanning the area for other movement. She said, "Impressive, guys. Nicely done."

Noack replied, "You, too, West. But no time to rest."

Chapter 34

While the guards by the road were being taken down, Grant, Caldwell and Driessen were positioned some 70 yards to one side of the house.

They could see two people on the front porch. However, activities inside remained a mystery, including what was happening to Jennifer.

Caldwell said, "You two are going to handle the shits on the front porch, while I go in that backdoor."

Both Grant and Driessen began to protest. But Paige stopped them. "Forget it. Charlie, you're not quick enough anymore, and Stephen, you've been working in a church. Enough said."

Grant was annoyed, but he knew she was right. "Fine," he replied coolly.

Driessen added, "As usual, your people skills leave something to be desired, Paige."

Caldwell continued, "Once we move, there's no cover. The two on the porch are either going to move back inside or make a break to get behind that car parked out front. You guys can't let that happen."

Driessen answered, "I get it. This ain't my first rodeo."

Caldwell said, "Let me get a head start, so when the shooting starts, I'm on the building."

Grant simply said, "Go."

As Paige moved into the night, Grant realized that his black clergy clothes would serve as an advantage compared even with the brown that both Paige and Charlie wore.

He looked at Driessen. "Let's go."

With guns out, Grant and Driessen moved at a jog, until the two kidnappers on the porch spotted them and moved for their weapons.

Driessen stopped to take aim. Stephen also brought his gun to bear on the targets, but he continued to move ahead at a slow walk.

Make the first shot count.

Grant settled on the man with long blond hair. He fired off four quick shots. Two hit home, stomach and chest. Ben, the blond kidnapper, fell back against the front door of the house. He bled out as the gunfight continued.

Thank you.

Driessen's shots missed their marks, so the other kidnapper, Carlos, dove behind the car. He left his AK47 behind, but still had a handgun. And now he had cover that Grant and Driessen did not.

He popped up from behind the silver sedan, fired two shots at the advancing Driessen and Grant, and then dropped down behind the vehicle.

Driessen hit the ground. He looked to his left, where Grant simply kept walking forward with his gun pointed. "Grant, what the hell are you doing?"

Carlos rose once again, and surprise flashed on his face as he realized that Grant was still walking at him.

Carlos got off a round, before Grant fired two that ricocheted off the car. The kidnapper dropped back down.

Grant simply kept walking dead ahead at a steady pace.

Lord, I've got to get to her.

Driessen got to his feet, and started moving at the vehicle as well. But he was far behind Grant, who was a mere 15 yards from the car.

Carlos popped up, and fired two wild shots. One caught flesh on Grant's left shoulder. Searing pain moved from the wound across his upper body, up his neck, and seized his head.

He wavered for a split second. But his relentless, apparently unstoppable walk proceeded.

Grant was on top of the car, and he stopped. He waited, unmoving.

On the other side, the kidnapper's eyes moved about frantically. He bit his lip. Carlos then took a deep breath, and started to push himself up with his legs.

Once the man's forehead emerged from behind the car, Stephen pulled the trigger.

At that range, the top of Carlos' head and part of his brain were ripped from the rest of his body, and splattered across the dirt and sand leading up to the house.

* * *

Once the gunfire started out front, Paige ran the remaining several yards to the backdoor.

Inside, Gil Rice was startled from a light sleep in the front room. The noise of a body hitting the front door stopped his movement in that direction.

He stood in the middle of the room. His head swung back and forth, but his feet remained planted.

As the next shots rang out, Rice looked at a variety of guns sitting on a table near the front door. He grabbed a SIG P229. His head turned again when he heard the creak of the backdoor.

More gun shots came from outside. Rice finally moved, grabbing the gun and heading back toward the hallway.

* * *

Paige cringed as the door made noise while it opened. She moved inside to a shabby kitchen, scanning the room. She moved quietly to the doorway on her left. As she led with her gun into the hallway, a shot sent her back into the kitchen.

* * *

Stephen continued moving past Carlos' body, without giving it a glance. He climbed the stairs, and as he was pushing aside the body leaning against the front door of the house with his foot, a shot rang out from inside.

He didn't hesitate. Grant opened the door, and moved into the room.

Gil Rice was leaning up against the wall, next to the hallway down which he had just fired a shot.

Grant had his Glock trained on his target's chest. "Drop the gun now, or I will drop you."

Rice obliged, and even put his hands in the air.

Grant called out, "Paige, you okay?"

"Yes."

Grant demanded, "Where's my wife?"

Rice replied, "Wife? You're the pastor?"

Before Grant could reply, Paige called out, "Stephen, in here, come quick!"

Grant bolted down the hallway, as Driessen came through the front door and took charge of Rice.

Stephen turned the corner into the second bedroom on the right. Paige was on her knees next to Jennifer.

He froze.

Paige said, "Her breathing is shallow, and her pulse is slow."

Grant slid to his wife's side. He didn't know what to do. Her face was caked with blood, and so swollen that she would not have been able to open her eyes even if conscious. Bruises populated most of the visible parts of her body. He gently stroked her hair. "Jen," he whispered. "What did they do?"

Paige got up, and switched channels on her radio. "Noack, are you there?"

"Yes, we're moving to the house, but scouting for others. Status? Is everyone all right?"

"Two hostiles dead. We've got another. Rest of us are okay. You need to get a copter now. Jennifer is..." She turned her back on Stephen, stepped into the hallway and moved to the front room. "She's not good. Get help quick."

"We're on it."

Paige looked at Driessen. She answered his unspoken question with a slight shake of the head.

In response, he said, "Crap."

She turned to Rice, who Driessen had put in a straight-back chair in the middle of the room. Caldwell pointed her gun, and asked, "Who the fuck are you, and why did you take Jennifer Grant?"

At the same time, down the hall, Stephen had ever so gently cut Jennifer's arms and legs free. He wiped away his own tears. His face was on the floor next to Jennifer's. "Jen, hold on, babe. Just please hold on."

He stared at his wife. He then got up and called out, "Charlie, get in here."

Driessen raised an eyebrow at Paige. She said, "Go ahead. I'll watch the dirt bag."

Driessen entered the bedroom, and halted when he saw Jennifer lying on the floor.

Grant brushed past without looking him in the eyes. "Stay with Jennifer."

Driessen's surprise was apparent. "Uh, well, okay. What are you...?"

Grant was blind with fury and hatred. He pushed reason aside. He had only allowed himself to go to such a place three times before in his entire life. And those were many years ago, certainly before becoming a pastor. Yet, even amidst the overwhelming anger, a small part of his mind worked on trying to justify what he was set on now doing. But no part urged him not to do it.

As he walked into the front room, Grant raised the Glock, pointing it at Rice.

Paige said, "Stephen?"

He held up his left hand to indicate that she should say nothing more, while his right had the gun trained on Rice.

"You were the one I spoke with on the phone."

Rice looked tired, resigned to a fate he had not expected. He replied, "Yes."

"You ran this operation?"

"Yes."

"Do you recall what I said on the phone?"

"Yes, you said that if I hurt her, you would kill me."

"Well, you hurt her, Mr....?"

"My name is Gil Rice. And I did this because your father-in-law killed my son. He..."

Grant knew he should have let him keep talking, but he simply did not care. His rage blurred everything. "Stop. I didn't ask you why you did this, Mr. Rice. All I know is that my wife is on the edge of death. Do you think that I will carry through on my pledge to kill you?"

Rice looked Grant in the eyes for several seconds. "If I was standing where you are right now, I would pull the trigger. So, yes, I think you will."

God, forgive me.

Grant said, "You're right, Mr. Rice, I am."

But before Grant could fire, a loud crack exploded next to him. A hole materialized in Gil Rice's forehead. Blood spewed forth. He toppled over backwards in the chair, and crashed lifeless to the floor.

Grant instinctively whirled his gun around at the source of the shot.

Paige lowered her weapon, and looked at Grant. "Stephen, are you going to shoot me?"

What the hell?

"What? Paige." He looked at Rice on the floor, and back at her. "Why? Why would you do that?"

Driessen arrived with gun drawn. "What the hell happened?" Paige shook her head at him. Charlie retreated, heading back to Jennifer.

Paige looked Stephen in the eyes. "I've seen that look before, Stephen. You were going to shoot him. I couldn't allow that. You can't do things like that anymore. But I can."

"What? No." *She shot him for ... me?*

Paige added, "We've saved each other before. This time, I had to save you from yourself." She slipped her gun into the small of her back, grabbed a t-shirt hanging on a nearby chair, and moved over to the table where assorted guns were resting. She picked up a small handgun by the barrel with the shirt, walked over to Rice's body, pressed his handprint on the weapon, and then dropped it next to the body.

Grant stood watching.

Paige raised the intensity in her voice. "Stephen, get in there with your wife. A medical helicopter is on the way."

Grant placed his own gun into the small of his back as well, between the black clergy shirt and his belt, and raced back to Jennifer.

When re-entering the bedroom, Stephen stopped, and looked Charlie in the eye this time. The two men silently passed each other – Stephen going to kneel next to Jennifer, and Charlie returning to Paige.

God, no matter what I've done, Jennifer's a victim. Please grant her healing.

Noack arrived. He looked around the room, stopping at Rice. "Some body count."

Caldwell answered, "It could have been worse." She hesitated, and then added, "Actually, it still could be."

Paige stepped out onto the porch, and looked up in the sky. A distant light grew brighter, and then sounds of whirling chopper blades could be heard.

Chapter 35

There was room for Stephen at Jennifer's side and among the FBI medics in the helicopter. But after touching down at the hospital in North Las Vegas, she was rushed away into surgery, and nurses tried to ferry Grant in a different direction in order to patch up his shoulder.

But he would not budge from the waiting room closest to where Jennifer was. His shoulder was treated, and then he suddenly was alone. At that point, the weight of Jennifer's injuries and his actions bore in far deeper than his wound.

Stephen thought about how his life had been transformed twice over the previous two decades.

First, Grant was called to serve Jesus as a pastor, leaving behind his work at the CIA. He relished his responsibilities as a SEAL and then with the CIA, along with the accomplishments. Grant knew that he had made a difference. But after resolving some of Grant's doubts, troubles and questions, the Lord made clear where he ultimately belonged.

Years later, when Jennifer came into his life in an unexpected way, Stephen found a love and closeness he previously thought was not possible on this earth.

Now, he sat staring at a tiled floor in a hospital, wondering if he was on the brink of losing these two great loves in his life.

But the more powerful impulse kept him focused on, and praying for, Jennifer.

Even while praying, though, his mind wandered – now to a new, profound guilt that he never experienced before.

I've told so many people that God will forgive. But this? How could God or Paige or Jennifer possibly forgive this?

No doubt existed in Grant's mind that he was going to pull that trigger. But Paige still knew him well enough to read what he was about to do. So, she did it for him.

Paige murdered Rice so I couldn't. What am I supposed to do with that?

Tears formed at the edges of his eyes.

He thought about the events in reverse order.

Paige fired the shot. He struggled with the enormous consequences, feeling deep regret. But there was something more.

Jennifer on the floor. Is she going to make it? Grant was immersed in sorrow. Again, though, there was more.

He didn't want to acknowledge what lurked in the dark corner of his mind.

Come on, at least be honest.

As Grant thought about what had been done to Jennifer, feelings of anger persisted, overwhelmingly centered on Gil Rice, but a small, nagging portion was directed at Paige.

Grant was angry that it was Paige, not him, that put a bullet in Rice's forehead.

He felt guilty about all of it. Yet, he still wanted to be the one who pulled the trigger. And if ever presented with such a horrendous scenario again, Grant knew that he would react in the same way. But he never again would allow anyone else to beat him to the trigger. He would take responsibility for his actions, and intentions.

How do I ask God to forgive what I still want to do, and would do again? And how do I thank Paige, and ask for her

*forgiveness? And what about Rice being killed while
unarmed?*

A few more tears formed, and slid down his cheeks.

*And what the hell is Jennifer going to say when I tell her
all of this? If I get to tell her.*

Grant shook his head, and bolted up from the chair,
hoping that the quick physical change might shake up
where he was mentally as well.

He pulled out his BlackBerry, and called Father Ron
McDermott. Grant needed the directness that only Ron
could offer.

Ron immediately asked, "Stephen, what's going on with
Jennifer?"

Stephen brought him up to date on Jennifer.

Ron replied, "Have the doctors said anything yet?"

"No, nothing." He paused. "Ron, I need to talk to
someone about what's happened."

"Of course, I'm here for both of you, whatever's needed."

"I know." Grant's voice went lower. "I need to tell you all
of it, in complete confidence."

Stephen went on to tell Ron every detail of what had
transpired at the ranch, as well as what he was wrestling
with sitting alone in the hospital.

When Grant finished, his friend replied, "My God,
Stephen, you've set the table for some serious therapy."

Grant managed to chuckle, which he knew was what his
friend was looking to achieve. "Yes, thanks for that."

Ron continued, "Stephen, I can't tell you that I
understand what you've gone through, nor can I assess
your decisions in a completely objective way. I've never
been there. Don't have a clue. But I can tell you three
things with complete confidence. First, Paige has put her
life on the line for you. That might not be new to the two of
you, given the hints you've provided as to your partnership
at the CIA, and when I saw you two in action. But that's
incredibly rare. My guess is that she'll not only forgive you,

but will be a bit perplexed as to why you're looking for forgiveness."

Grant only managed, "Maybe."

"Second, you risked everything for Jennifer, and it's apparent even to this unmarried Catholic priest that she cares for you deeply and fully. I'm about as sure as a human being can be about predicting the actions of another human being when I say that Jennifer will forgive. As a matter of fact, she also might be a bit bewildered as to why you need forgiveness."

Stephen tried to reply, but he couldn't. He simply cleared his throat.

Ron proceeded, "And finally, I have absolute confidence in our Lord's forgiveness. Take it all to Him, put it at His feet, confess what needs to be confessed, and I know that you will be forgiven."

Stephen mustered, "I sure hope so, my friend."

The sinless Christ died for my sins. Paige sinned to stop me from sinning?

"That's what we all hope for, Stephen," answered Ron. "But it's more than hope. It's what we have confidence in."

The door at the other end of the room opened, and in walked Dixon Shaw.

Stephen said to Ron, "I've got to go, Jen's father just arrived."

"Remember, Stephen, you're not alone."

"Thanks, Ron."

"You're welcome. Give us news when you can."

Dix had lost the charm on display when Stephen first met him. He now looked older than his sixty-plus years.

Stephen was surprised when Shaw gave him a tight hug. When he pulled back, Dix asked, "How's our Jenny?"

"I don't know, Dix."

"I heard a little bit about what happened from Agent Noack. That this Rice had to be shot when he pulled a gun on your friend, Ms. Caldwell." He shook his head. "I'm glad the fucking bastard is dead."

Grant replied, "Me, too."

Dix raised an eyebrow slightly at Grant's response.

Stephen decided not to bring up what Rice had said about Dix killing his son. It was time for Grant to get back to thinking about and praying for his wife.

The two men sat in silence waiting to hear the fate of the woman who linked them together. They both loved Jennifer in very different ways that went far beyond one being a husband and the other a father.

Chapter 36

After he hung up with Stephen, Father Ron McDermott worked the phones with those closest to Stephen and Jennifer.

Ron obviously refrained from relaying the confidential part of his conversation with Stephen. But he brought each friend up to speed as to the basics of what had happened to Jennifer.

An hour and a half later, just after noon on Friday, Ron had managed to gather Tom and Maggie Stone, Cara Stone, Joan and George Kraus, and Zack Charmichael in the living room of the rectory at St. Luke's Catholic Church.

They began with bowed heads and prayer.

Ron led the group. "Lord Jesus Christ, most Holy Redeemer, you make all things new. We bring our dear friends Jennifer and Stephen before you. Renew Jennifer, and heal her with your love. Please help both of them face and overcome their fears. Be with them when they feel alone. Comfort them. And send your Word, as it heals and delivers from all destructions. Touch their bodies and the depths of their souls, cleansing, purifying, restoring them to wholeness and strength for service in Your Kingdom. Amen."

The others repeated the "Amen."

Questions flowed for which none of them had any real answers.

Zack finally moved to focus the discussion. "Listen, I've decided to open St. Mary's to a round-the-clock prayer vigil for Jennifer and Stephen. I'm asking parishioners to come at any time starting at three today. My plan is to have time for personal prayer, scriptural passages and devotional readings. I'll make sure that at least someone is always there, but as news spreads, I don't think we're going to have any problem with an empty church."

Tom said, "That's a wonderful idea, Zack. You can count on us to come."

"Absolutely," added Maggie. She offered a sad smile to Zack, while brushing back her shoulder-length, strawberry-blond hair behind her right ear.

On the deep, plush couch, next to Maggie and Tom sat Joan, with George's arm around her shoulder. The news about her best friend had hit Joan hard. The red in her large blue eyes almost matched her near-orange hair, and the dark circles under those eyes looked worse given her pale skin. Normally a cutting-edge fashion plate and outgoing personality, Joan would outshine George with his cautious ways and conservative clothes. But not today, as she was in the same light gray t-shirt and black sweat pants she had on when hearing about Jen late last night. Joan clearly was carrying a heavy heart for her friend.

She interrupted the discussion. "Zack, I think that's great as well. But I can't stay here. I'm flying out to Vegas later this afternoon. I have to be with Jennifer."

Tom said, "I understand, Joan. But do you want to wait until we hear more?"

"No. What difference does it make? Either way, good or bad news..." Her voice broke.

George squeezed her shoulder.

Joan took a deep breath. She continued, "I need to be there. George is going to stay with the girls." They had two teenage daughters.

George nodded in agreement.

Ron broke a brief silence. "You're right, Joan. I'm going to fly out with you, if you don't mind."

She smiled. "Mind? Of course not, Ron. Thank you."

Tom said, "All right. Maggie and I will stay here, and help Zack at St. Mary's."

Cara, who looked in most ways like a younger version of her mother, though with longer strawberry-blond hair, added, "I'll be helping Zack, too, of course."

Sitting in a chair next to hers, Zack took Cara's hand.

Chapter 37

Paige and Charlie walked through the swinging white doors of the hospital waiting room.

After glancing at Shaw, Paige went straight to Stephen. "Any news?"

"Nothing."

When they hugged, Paige whispered, "Does he know what Rice said?"

Stephen shook his head ever so slightly.

Shaw was on his feet, and Stephen introduced him to Paige and Charlie.

In a somber tone, Dix said, "I want to thank both of you for helping to rescue Jennifer."

Paige smiled, while Charlie grunted, "Sure."

The four sat down. Awkward silence reigned for a few minutes until the other set of doors from the operating room swung open. The four rose in unison.

A tall black man with tightly cut hair in blue hospital attire asked, "Mr. Grant?"

"Yes, I'm Stephen Grant. How is Jennifer, doctor? How is my wife?" Grant felt like he couldn't breathe.

"I'm Dr. Adrian Harper, head of neuro-surgery. Your wife was badly beaten, as you know. We had to patch up some bleeding in her abdomen, but her main problem is bleeding and pressure on the brain. We were able to relieve some of that pressure, and we've started her on anti-swelling medications. Mr. Grant, right now, Jennifer is in a coma, and we're moving her into ICU."

"Coma?" replied Grant.

Dix interrupted, "What does that mean, doctor? Is she going to make it?"

Harper looked at Shaw. "And you are?"

"I'm Dix Shaw, Jennifer's father."

"Mr. Shaw, I'm sorry. I didn't recognize you. Jennifer is out of immediate danger. But..."

It was Stephen's turn to interject. "What does 'out of immediate danger' mean exactly?"

"Gentlemen, we got Jennifer just in time to save her life. Brain damage combined with a coma make for an uncertain prognosis. Fortunately, though, we've seen dramatic improvements in assorted treatments in recent years. But at this point, we have incomplete information about what's going on in her head."

Dix demanded, "What are the possibilities here, doctor? What about permanent brain damage?"

Stephen clenched his teeth.

Harper looked from Shaw to Grant, and then back to Shaw. "I know it's frustrating. But I cannot answer that, and you don't want to start thinking that way. Right now, we're focused on taking care of Mrs. Grant, and getting her moving in the right direction."

Grant knew they were not going to get any more from Harper. "Thank you for all that you have done and are doing for Jennifer, Dr. Harper. When can I see her?"

"Give us a little time to get her set. A nurse will come out to get you when we're ready."

After Harper left, Dix said, "He needs to tell us what Jenny's in for here."

Stephen replied, "He can't. They don't know enough at this point."

Dix kept pushing. "But what are the possibilities?"

With his emotions raw, Grant's anger flared up. "Dix, you want to know the possibilities? Jennifer could come out of this thing in an hour, in days, in weeks, or never. She might suffer no brain damage, or have permanent disabilities. And right now, they're hooking her up to IVs, monitors, catheters, and probably a ventilator to make sure that her comatose brain doesn't translate into failed breathing. Those are the realities and the possibilities."

Grant could see the anger rising on Dix's face as well. The room suddenly felt very cramped.

Dix said, "How do you know so damn much about this?"

"Because as Paige can tell you, I wound up in a coma many years ago after being beaten to a pulp, much like Jennifer. I came out of it in a week."

Dix looked at Paige, and then back to Stephen. Shaw then declared, "I need to get some air for a few minutes."

Stephen sat down, and felt the brief adrenaline hit wane.

Paige sat next to him, and Charlie across from the two.

Referring to Dix, Stephen said, "I understand his frustration. It's the not knowing."

Paige replied, "Yes, it is."

Stephen looked at her. "I didn't understand what you went through back then."

"That was a long time ago, Stephen. A different life, it seems."

"It does seem like that."

Grant thought about how different it, in fact, was. Paige had been much more than a partner. They were lovers, but not really in love in a full, commitment sense, at least not how Grant understood love and commitment today. But it was as close as love got. And when Paige had re-entered his life just a few years ago, before his falling in love and marrying Jennifer, he briefly entertained the possibility of a complete love with Paige. But that was not meant to be.

Now, they sat next to each other as friends, but a friendship with a rare depth – where one friend was willing to not only risk her life to save the other's spouse, but also to save that friend from committing a grave sin by committing that sin herself.

Grant wrestled with why Paige would do all of this. Was it friendship? Most friends would not do what she had done.

Was it because she still had feelings as a lover for him? He quickly decided such a thought was nothing more than flattering himself. Holding on to something that she knew was done was not Paige Caldwell.

He settled on the idea that their previous partnership, protection of each other, and yes, intimacy had transformed into a love as friends. Paige had a firm understanding that Stephen was fully committed to and in love with Jennifer.

Of course, Grant understood that Paige's ultimate motivations would remain a mystery. He also knew that he was a rare, blessed man to love and be loved by two smart, beautiful, caring, though very different women – one as a spouse and the other as a friend.

Grant stood up, and said, "You two don't need to stay here. You need to decompress and get some rest."

"That's okay, Grant," replied Charlie.

"No, it's not, Charlie."

Paige moved to her feet as well. "All right, Stephen. We'll get cleaned up and eat. But after that we're going to look into the two unsolved parts of this attack on Jennifer. Who the hell was Rice talking to here in Vegas? And what's the deal with Rice's comment that he did this because your father-in-law killed his son?"

A wave of guilt and regret hit Grant again. Stephen said, "We ... I should have gotten that out of Rice before..."

Paige observed, "It's done. We did what we did. Let's move on. The FBI is on these questions, too. And we've got

Sean poking into it all. We'll get something, and then get whatever other bastard or bastards are involved." She turned to the door, and said, "Let's go, Charlie."

Charlie said, "Grant, you concentrate on your wife. We'll concentrate on closing this thing out."

As Charlie followed Paige out of the room, Stephen was left alone, once more, trying to sort through myriad thoughts, questions, and emotions.

Chapter 38

On the way down to the hospital lobby, Paige and Charlie were discussing where they should check in to get showers, eat, and set up some kind of base of operations.

As they exited the front of the building, Paige spotted Shaw talking on his phone. She told Charlie, "I think we can get some very nice accommodations." Paige strolled up to Shaw, and inquired as to where he recommended they stay.

As expected, Shaw insisted they be his guests at Casino Beach. After a faux protest, Paige accepted on behalf of Charlie and herself.

Less than an hour later, Paige had stripped off her clothes, stepped into a large, waterfall shower, and lathered her body with cocoa butter soap. She lingered under the water for nearly twenty minutes.

She then slipped into a rich, white terrycloth robe, and picked up the phone to order room service. "I know it's 9:30 in the morning, but can I order dinner?"

After being assured that since she was a valued guest at the Casino Beach Vegas Resort, Paige was told she could order anything she liked, even off-menu.

While waiting for the food, she poured herself a Malibu rum and Diet Coke in an ice-filled glass, and sank into a thickly cushioned, white chair. Paige sipped the drink, and sighed when her phone rang.

Paige moved across to the bedroom, where she had dropped her computer attaché, duffle bag, clothes, and the phone.

She looked at the screen. "Hello, Sean."

In his low, raspy voice, McEnany asked, "Paige, how are you?"

"I'm in a spacious suite at a resort. Just finished a long shower, slipped into a comfortable robe, and made myself a Malibu and Diet Coke. Now, I'm waiting for grilled swordfish to arrive at my room."

"Sounds like things have improved from a few hours ago."

"Nowhere to go but up."

"Okay, but I'm not sure that mixed drinks before ten in the morning is a good idea."

"What time is it there in Santo Domingo?"

"Nearly one."

"Well, then, just think of it as having lunch local, and you don't have to worry about me drinking in the morning."

"Fair enough. Anything more on Jennifer?"

Paige gave him what she knew, and then asked, "What about you, anything on Rice?"

"Yes, and his team as well." He summed up the backgrounds of Rice and the four men who had worked with him. "There's no prior link between those four and Rice. They moved in different universes. The four were linked to organized crime in the western continental U.S., while he was a prison guard in Chicago with a competent, yet unimpressive record of service."

As Paige listened, she finished her drink, walked over to the bar, and mixed another. "What about through the prison?"

McEnany continued, "Maybe, but it's hard to see. While he had nothing of distinction in his record, there were no problems either. Seemed like a guy who punched in, did his job, kept his head down, and punched out. The Gil Rice story looks like he got word about his son gone missing, came to Vegas, and knocked around for months apparently trying to figure out who killed his son. After being quiet for some time, he recently sold his house, and used the cash to lease that ranch. And based on some of his last words, Rice got information that Shaw was the one who killed his son."

Paige asked, "What about the son?"

McEnany gave the history of Ollie Rice, from blackjack dealer with disciplinary issues to missing person, presumed murdered, body never found, and eventually a cold case.

"Anything else?" asked Paige.

"Definitely. To throw a wild card in this mix, I was pulling in some favors and got a hit on somebody from Stephen's past, and yours."

"Who?"

"Eric Clark."

"Clark. No shit?"

McEnany reported, "I found out that he's in WITSEC and living somewhere in the Las Vegas area."

"I knew he went into witness protection. Under what name?"

"I haven't gotten that yet. My source is reluctant. You think it's a coincidence that Clark's around?"

"I'm not big on coincidences," answered Paige.

Chapter 39

After getting dressed, Caldwell gave Charlie Driessen the rundown on what Sean had said. She then left Charlie at the hotel, and arrived at the hospital just as Stephen had left Jennifer's side in ICU.

Grant's energy level was fluctuating wildly. Objectively, he knew that he needed to find time for a little sleep. But that didn't mean he was going to do so.

Paige sat down directly across from him in the waiting room. "How is she?"

"No change, at least in terms of what they're telling me. It's hard to see her like that. Her face is so swollen, and all of those tubes." He swallowed hard.

"I know."

They sat quietly for a couple of minutes.

Stephen looked directly in Paige's eyes. "Listen, thank you for all you've done, for coming, for putting it all on the line."

"You're welcome. But I couldn't do anything less for you. I know you wouldn't do less for me."

He let that sink in, and then added, "And about Gil Rice..."

The name, and what happened, hung in the air between them.

Stephen continued, "Can I be straight with you, Paige?"

"You better be."

"I'm sorry."

Paige offered a small laugh. "What the hell are you sorry for?"

"I put you in a situation with no good option, no right choice, because you knew what I was going to do."

"Of course, I knew. I could see it on your face. Saw it a long time ago. But you're in a different place now, with different responsibilities."

"I know, and that's why I'm sorry."

"Stop with the 'sorry.' There's no reason to be sorry. For what he did to Jennifer, he got exactly what he deserved," Paige declared in straightforward fashion.

Stephen decided not to delve more deeply into that. But he added, "Well, in addition to feeling guilty about the position I put you in, I also confess to being a bit angry."

"I know."

"You know?"

"Yes." She leaned back in the chair, crossed her legs, and folded her arms. "It's simple. Even though you're a pastor today, there's still some part of the Stephen Grant I worked with in there." She pointed at him. "And you're pissed that I was the one who shot the son of a bitch who hurt your wife."

Right.

He offered no verbal reply.

Paige said, "If you're done apologizing for crap that you shouldn't be apologizing for, I have some information." She proceeded to fill Grant in on what McEnany had said about Rice and his four partners, then finished up with the revelation on Eric Clark.

Stephen said, "Clark. No Shit?"

"That's exactly what I said. And yes, no shit. We don't know his new name or exact location, yet. I've no doubt, however, that Sean will find all of that out shortly."

"Thank Sean for me."

The two turned as Dixon Shaw walked through the doors from the ICU.

Stephen whispered, "Time to put Dix to the test?"

Paige nodded.

Shaw sat down a couple of seats away from Paige. "They kicked me out. We're supposed to leave her alone with them for a while."

Stephen said, "Dix, I need to ask you something."

"Yes, Pastor, what is it?"

"Cutting to the chase. Before Gil Rice died, he said that he did this because you had killed his son."

"What? He said I killed his son? That's crazy."

Paige interjected, "Then why would he say it?"

"Why would he say it?" Dix elevated his voice. "How the fuck do I know why that crazy piece of shit said that? Look at what he did to my daughter. How the hell do I explain that either?"

Stephen said, "Okay, what about the guys he was working with?" Stephen gave the rundown on what Sean had found, emphasizing the organized crime links.

Dix said, "Never heard of them before. I wish I had. Then I'd have more to go on to get whoever else was involved in this. And then I'd do to them exactly what you, Ms. Caldwell, did to Gil Rice."

Paige smirked, and looked at Stephen.

Stephen took the next step uneasily. He threw out the name Eric Clark, saying this person might be somehow involved. "Know him? Ever hear of him?"

Shaw said, "No, I don't know an Eric Clark."

Throughout the exchange, Grant had watched every move by Shaw, measured his voice, and watched his eyes. He knew that Paige was doing the same. Both Stephen and Paige watched Dixon Shaw amidst silence.

Shaw stood up. "Have I passed your test, Pastor?"

Stephen thought about how he should respond. He wanted to say, "For now." But instead, he lied. "Of course, Dix. Sorry if you thought this was some kind of a test."

"Yeah, right," replied Dix. "I'll be back."

He left the room.

Stephen asked Paige, "What do you think?"

She answered, "I think we should have Sean do an in-depth look at your father-in-law."

Chapter 40

While weaving through traffic in his yellow, blacktop Ferrari California 30 from the hospital to Casino Beach, Shaw called and instructed both Two Gloves Geraci and Chet Easton to be waiting in his personal conference room for him.

All traces of law enforcement had been removed from Shaw's suite.

After getting a kiss and hug from Candy, and relaying to her the latest about Jennifer, Dix told Candy that he needed to speak with Nicky and Chet alone. She headed off to the gym.

His two partners were waiting for Dix at the long table.

"Even when I heard the name Gil Rice, I still didn't want to know. But now, I have to. Let's hear exactly what the fuck happened with Ollie Rice." Dix was staring at Nicky.

Two Gloves said, "You're fine. We're fine. I worked him over a bit, just to scare him off. And then the little shit has some kind of seizure or heart attack, something. All of a sudden, he's dead. Trust me, we didn't do anything that should have killed him."

"And?"

"And what do you think, Dix? The body disappeared, and it's – what? – eight months later, and no one will ever find the body. It's a done deal."

"Done deal?" Dix smashed his fist down on the table. "Obviously not. Apparently before he bought it, Gil Rice said that he kidnapped and beat Jennifer because I had killed his son."

Chet Easton squirmed in his seat, but remained silent.

Two Gloves asked, "And that's all he said?"

"As far as I know, that was it."

"Then what's the fucking difference, Dix? He ain't breathing no more. Like I said, done deal."

"Again, with the 'done deal.' Rice was working with somebody, and that somebody is the person tying Ollie Rice's death to me." He looked from Geraci to Easton, and back to Geraci. "To us, gentlemen."

Easton shifted in his chair, again.

Geraci said, "Hmmm, yeah, I see what you mean."

"Well, I'm glad you now see the obvious." Dix turned to Chet. "Find out who the hell was working with Rice, and quick. We have to get to that person before the feds or my son-in-law's friends do."

Chet replied, "Sure, Dix."

Geraci added, "You're right."

"Of course, I'm right. Now both of you get the hell out, and get answers."

After Geraci and Easton left the suite, Dix pulled out a smartphone, and punched in seven digits.

He said, "Gino, it's me. I've got a priority one task."

Gino said, "What is it, sir?"

"I assume you've been following what's happened with my daughter?"

"Of course, sir."

Dix relayed what Geraci said. "You need to find out how Gil Rice traced this back to me. Look at the four who worked with him." He gave the names. "Look at a man named Eric Clark. Look at everything."

"Yes, sir."

Chapter 41

Other than special surprises from Jennifer, Stephen Grant generally was not a person especially fond of the unexpected.

Given the current chaos, though, his spirits rose when Joan Kraus and Father Ron McDermott walked into the hospital waiting room.

Joan, her eyes filled with tears, came up and hugged Stephen tightly.

Without loosening her grip, she asked, "How is she, Stephen?"

"Jen's in a coma, Joan."

"Oh, God..." Her knees buckled, but Stephen held onto her, and guided her gently to a chair.

Stephen knelt in front of her. "Joan, are you okay?"

She let a burst of tears flow, and then breathed in deeply. "Stephen, a coma? What does that mean?"

Stephen was unable to provide a satisfactory answer because he still did not know himself. He spoke of time, an unknown amount, and the hope that this would allow her to heal.

As she tried to find a tissue in her pocketbook, Stephen rose to finally greet Ron. Grant was taken off guard by his friend's moist eyes. Stephen could not recall seeing Ron come close to a tear. In turn, Stephen had to struggle even more to tamp down the urge to further unleash his emotions. The two men hugged.

Stephen said, "Thanks for coming, my friend."

"Of course. I think Tom wanted to come, but he's helping Zack."

"Helping Zack?"

"Yes, your protégé has a prayer vigil going at St. Mary's for Jennifer. Well, actually, for both of you."

Stephen felt a wave of appreciation for all of his friends at home, and now here. "I haven't got word back home since I spoke with you. When was that? This morning. I'm so sorry."

Ron smiled. "Under the circumstances, I think you can be forgiven."

Stephen's mind jumped to seeing Gil Rice tumbling back with a bloody hole in his head, and Paige holding the gun. *Forgiven?*

Grant refocused. He offered Joan and Ron what little more information he had about Jennifer, including that her blood pressure was still low, her heartbeat slow, and that she was on a ventilator.

A nurse poked her head in the room, saying, "Pastor Grant, you can come back in."

He said, "Thank you. Do you mind if Joan comes in with me?"

The nurse asked, "Family?"

Stephen looked at Joan and her pleading eyes. "Of course, this is my wife's sister, Joan Kraus."

Not technically true, but de facto.

The nurse said, "Yes, but both of you cannot stay too long. It'll have to be one at a time after this."

Joan managed a small smile, and murmured, "Thank you so much."

Before moving, Stephen turned to Ron, and asked, "Could you call...?"

"I'll get a hold of Tom, Zack and George. Don't worry."

"Thanks, Ron."

As they moved to the doors leading into ICU, Joan and Stephen were leaning on each other for support.

Chapter 42

During the earliest minutes of Saturday morning on Long Island, some 25 people were spread out amongst the pews of St. Mary's Lutheran Church.

Fifteen had arrived just in the last few minutes, after receiving the church-wide email no more than a half hour prior that Jennifer Grant was in a coma.

Pastor Zack Charmichael stood next to Barbara Tunney, the longtime, super-efficient church secretary at St. Mary's, looking out the window of his office at the arriving cars.

The gray-haired Barbara pushed the glasses up on her nose, and started buttoning one of her church sweaters that hung over her traditional flowered dress. "Just when you have your doubts about St. Mary's, people come out in the middle of the night for a prayer vigil when one of our own is in distress."

Zack said, "It says a lot about Jennifer, and what she means to people here."

"I agree, not to mention Stephen and you as well."

Zack picked up his *Lutheran Service Book* from the desk, and said, "I'm going to go into the sanctuary. Time to relieve Glenn."

Glenn Oliver, a short, thin, easy-going black man who just turned sixty, was one of those critical volunteers needed for a church to run smoothly. He not only headed up the buildings and ground committee, but also often served as a Communion steward. Glenn was a widower. He retired from a career as a compliance officer on Wall Street to take care of his wife during a battle with cancer, which she eventually lost.

Zack moved down the hallway, through a door to the narthex, and then looked left into the sanctuary.

The inside of St. Mary's sanctuary nicely complemented the building's tudor exterior. Four-foot high, dark wood paneling lined the outside walls. That wood matched the pews, the Communion rail, and beams that ran into the peaks of the off-white ceilings. The windows, which came to points similar to the ceiling and ends of the pews, offered etchings of key points in the life of Jesus Christ. High above the altar hung a large Crucifix, and above the choir loft at the other end was a large window with Jesus as the teacher etched into it.

When Zack peered in, Glenn had just finished several readings from the Psalms done in responsive fashion. He then announced from the lectern, "Why don't we take 15 minutes or so for private prayer. To help, if you would like, selections of prayers and devotions have been printed out, and are in each pew. God bless."

Glenn turned and bowed at the altar. He then pivoted back around, and moved down the center aisle.

When Glenn entered the narthex, Zack said, "Thanks again, Glenn, for your help."

"No need for thanks. Jennifer is a close friend, not to mention a classy lady."

"That she is. Are you heading home?"

"No, I'm going to stay a while longer."

"Barbara just set out coffee, tea and some pastries in the conference room."

Glenn smiled. "Of course she did."

"Grab something. I'm going to announce it to everyone else in a few minutes."

Glenn headed in the direction of the coffee, while Zack moved into the sanctuary. He sat behind two leaders of the current church council. Everett Birk was the very large church president with a flattop, thin beard and mustache. Suzanne Maher, the council vice president, was both a prickly stickler on doctrine and much else, while also being a generous, elegant, spry elderly woman.

The front door of the church opened, and Zack glanced over his shoulder. When he saw that it was Beatrice Aiken, he immediately got to his feet and walked back to meet her.

Zack asked, "Bee, are you okay? What are you doing here, especially at this time?"

She looked at him a bit bewildered. "I'm not sure. I read the email... the prayer vigil for Jennifer ..."

"Why don't you come and sit in my office for a few minutes? Then you can go in and pray."

"You don't mind?"

"Of course not."

"No, I shouldn't bother you, not with everything going on with Jennifer."

Zack reassured, "Bee, really, it's all right. Come on."

As they walked slowly down the hallway, Glenn was sipping coffee and holding a Lady Finger cookie at the table set up by Barbara. He put both down, and offered his sympathies to Beatrice over the loss of Jay. She thanked him weakly, and then Zack pointed her to the most comfortable chair in his office.

Beatrice looked across the desk at him, and said, "I needed to come down here to church, to get out of the house."

"What is it, Bee?"

"My sister, Blair. She's been telling me over and over again that I can contact Jay."

"Contact Jay?"

"Yeah, you know, like through a psychic." She paused. "That doesn't feel right. Seems weird. I mean, we haven't even buried..." Her voice broke. She took a deep breath. "But if there's any chance..." She was clearly looking to Zack for guidance.

"You're right to be uneasy. I assume your sister is trying to help. But a psychic, Bee, is not going to help."

She asked, "What's the worst case?"

"That they mislead people, move them away from Christ and His Church." He paused for a moment. "Bee, all kinds of things pop into our minds after losing someone. You've lost Jay, *and* you're about to have a baby. I honestly can't fully comprehend what you're going through. But I'm guessing you want something real, reliable to grab onto, right? Something to help. Something that's sure. You want to know that Jay is with you, somehow. Right?"

Tears streamed down her face. "God, yes."

Zack continued, "Do you know why our Communion rail is a half circle? You know, it starts at the wall, circles around the altar, and then ends on the other side, but at the same wall."

She shook her head.

"It's done that way in some churches to remind us that Communion is not just about bringing together those of us at the rail at that moment in time. It's about Heaven and Earth coming together through Jesus Christ. It's about Christ's body and blood binding believers together across time and space, including those we've lost here on Earth. It's complete, with all the saints, angels and archangels. We are, in a very real sense, together with them during the Lord's Supper. That includes Jay, and others we've lost in death, but who live in Christ. There's no reason to turn to psychics when faith and hope come alive at the Communion rail during the Lord's Supper. At that rail, the real presence of Jesus – real, reliable and sure – unites us.

That's a staggering, powerful thing. To me, it's very reassuring."

Tears resumed, but this time they came with a small, sad smile. Beatrice said, "I never heard that before. That's really beautiful."

Zack smiled back.

She dabbed her eyes with a tissue, and said, "I think I'll go into the church now, and try to pray for ... you know ... for the first time since the accident."

"I'll join you, Bee," replied Zack.

As Zack walked with Bee, Cara Stone entered the building. She hugged Beatrice, and the three entered the sanctuary together.

Chapter 43

Midnight crept closer on Friday night in Las Vegas.

Stephen had been up for nearly 42 hours, and they ranked, to say the least, among the most taxing 42 hours of his life – which, given what he had done and faced during his adult years, was saying something.

As he sat, thought and prayed next to Jennifer in the ICU, Stephen pushed back against the mounting threat of sleep, deciding that he would have to surrender to caffeine.

He gently touched her hand, and said, "I'll be back, Jen. I'm sure Joan will be in while I get something caffeinated."

Stephen had no idea if it somehow helped to bring her back from the coma, but over the last few hours, he periodically spoke out loud to his wife. At the very least, it helped him, and the nurses seemed to approve.

When he entered the waiting room, Joan sprang to her feet, followed by Ron. Stephen said he had nothing new to report. He added, "Joan, why don't you go in with Jennifer, and maybe Ron and I can go downstairs for coffee, or some other caffeinated beverage?"

Stephen noticed the glance that Joan gave Ron, who responded with a slight nod.

A few minutes later, as they walked along the hospital's shiny floors, Stephen asked, "So, what was the nod about?"

Ron spoke plainly, as usual. "You've been though hell, and there's more to come. It's time for you to go back to the hotel, and get some sleep."

Before Stephen could utter his protest, Ron continued, "And by the way, please take a shower before you get ripe."

Stephen replied, "You're funny. There's no way that I'm leaving Jennifer right now."

"I don't care if you were some kind of Jack Bauer years ago. You're not today. More than, what, forty hours and counting?"

"It doesn't matter. I can..."

Ron grabbed his arm to stop him before entering the small hospital restaurant. He lowered his voice. "Stop the crap, Stephen. You're not thinking clearly. You know how long this could be."

"Or not be," Stephen interjected irritably.

"Yes, or not be. But the point is, as you've said, we just don't know. After what you've been through, lesser men than Stephen Grant would have crumbled, physically and emotionally. But even Stephen Grant is human."

Too human.

Ron persisted, "Joan and I came for both of you. And that means, since we're here, you need to get a shower, at least a few hours of sleep and even something respectable to eat."

He's right, of course. I'll be no good to Jen if I don't. But it doesn't feel right.

Stephen stood down. "Okay, Ron. I'm going to take your advice, and head back to the hotel for a few hours. But..."

Ron nodded, and said, "Yes, I'll call immediately if anything changes. Now go."

While in a taxi for the short ride to The Twenties, Grant couldn't shut off his brain. He pulled out his phone and called Paige.

"Hey, Grant, how's your wife?"

"No change, Charlie. And why are you answering Paige's phone?"

"Trading off some time, so we can each get a little rest. You know the drill."

"Yeah, I'm on my way to the hotel now to do the same."

"Good. Your friends are with Jennifer?"

"Yes."

"Okay. What are you calling about?"

"Any word on Clark yet, who he is now, or where he is?"

"I haven't been able to get anything. We're waiting to hear back from McEnany."

Grant started thinking out loud. "And who the hell was on the other end of that call somewhere around the hotel with Rice? What about Rice saying that Jennifer's father killed his son? And, again, how does any of that relate to Clark?"

"Lots of possibilities, and a few that I'm sure you don't want to think about in terms of your father-in-law. But it's all speculation. I got nothing."

Grant added, "Eric Clark and Dixon Shaw. How and what could that be?"

"Hell, could be nothing but coincidence, or it could be something more disturbing. We'll figure it out. Noack and his feds are on it. The local guys, too. Go back to your room, have a drink, go to sleep, and we'll let you know when we get something."

"Thanks again, Charlie."

"Yeah, sure."

Chapter 44

An array of television weathermen had announced that the record high temperature for April in Las Vegas was at risk. Triple digits had never been registered before in April, but 100°F would be in play for Vegas on this Saturday.

Though it was only 6:30 in the morning, Dixon Shaw had been awake for some two hours, staring at the ceiling of his bedroom for most of that time.

Candy stirred next to him. She rolled over, and stretched an arm across his chest. "Dix, you okay?"

"Sure, baby."

"Any word on Jennifer?"

"I called the hospital a couple of hours ago. No change. And I haven't heard from the Pastor."

They laid in silence for a couple minutes, then Candy said, "I've prayed for her, for Jennifer, Dix."

"That's good, Candy. I appreciate it."

She repositioned herself, resting her chin on the salt-and-pepper hair on his chest, and looked into his eyes. "Do you pray, Dix?"

"What?"

She repeated the question in matter-of-fact fashion. "Do you pray? I mean, have you prayed for Jennifer?"

"What do you mean?"

Candy gave a quizzical look. "What do you mean what do I mean? Do you ever talk to God? You know, ask Him for something, or thank Him?"

Dix leaned his head forward, and kissed Candy on the forehead. "It's funny that you ask that now. I'm not much for talking to God. I can only remember praying – if you can even call it that – twice in my life. I said thank you when Jenny was born, and then all these years later, I asked God to protect her when she was kidnapped."

Candy turned her head, and laid it sideways on his chest. With a touch of sadness in her voice, she replied, "Just those two times?"

"Yeah, like I said, I'm not much for praying."

The phone Dix had called Gino on sprang to life with a loud ring.

Dix said, "Sorry, baby, I've got to answer this."

Candy rolled away as Dix grabbed the phone and walked out of the room.

He answered the call. "Gino, what do you have?"

"Well, sir, that name you gave me – Eric Clark. He's in witness protection. Goes by the name Donnie Goodman. He was put there almost 20 years ago by your son-in-law."

"Grant?"

"Yes. It looks like Clark was behind your daughter's kidnapping. He was CIA, but helped run an antiquities smuggling ring out of Turkey. Grant and someone named Paige Caldwell brought him down. Clark gave up whom he worked for. The fact that a CIA officer was involved was kept quiet. Clark became Goodman. He lives in Vegas, works for the city, and cooked this up, apparently, to get revenge on Grant and get at your money."

"You're sure?"

"No doubt, sir. He's the guy. I've got an electronic trail on the money, and other links between Clark, Gil Rice, and three of the men working with Rice."

"You've got a location on this guy?"

"Yes, sir."

Dix demanded, "Give it to me, now."

Chapter 45

Still in the team's Santo Domingo house, Sean McEnany returned from the refrigerator with a bottled water.

He slipped a headset on, hit a few keys on the computer, and sipped the water while listening to the ringing of a distant phone.

A voice with an unmistakable note of annoyance answered, "Yes."

"Jonas, how's your day so far?" asked McEnany.

"Busier than I had planned for an early Saturday morning."

"Given how well you're compensated, I'm not about to apologize."

"Hey, I'd still like to get some time in with the kids."

"Right. Do you have what I need on Clark?"

"You know, Sean, I've given you a lot of valuable information over the years."

"Yes, you have, Jonas. Again, I believe our appreciation has been illustrated quite clearly, in a variety of forms, from money to making sure that your – how have we put it – checkered past remains hidden to all who matter in your life."

"Okay, okay. But WITSEC? This presents a different kind of delving and exposing. The DoJ takes this crap pretty seriously."

Sean smiled, shook his head, and took another slug of water.

"Sean, did you hear me? Are you there?"

"I heard, Jonas. You made your point. Trust me."

Jonas said, "Fine. Eric Clark is now one Donald Goodman."

Sean said, "Thanks, Jonas. This was important. I appreciate the help."

"You're welcome. But hold on a minute. I've got more."

"Yes?"

"Since you're a generous guy that I can always count on, I thought you'd appreciate knowing that you're not the only person in the market regarding Eric Clark, aka, Mr. Goodman."

Chapter 46

Once Sean McEnany found out that Eric Clark was Donald Goodman, it was child's play to get the rest of the information.

He was on the phone with Caldwell in less than an hour and a half.

McEnany provided a quick, but comprehensive rundown on where Clark lived, worked, his credit rating, bank accounts, extensive gambling habits and general gambling success, his preferred stops on the Internet, and that most people apparently called him Donnie.

Caldwell asked, "Do we know who this other person is looking at Clark?"

"My contact was not offering names."

"Shit. And you don't see anything unusual in Clark's bank accounts and financials?"

"Pretty boring, at least in terms of what I can see. He definitely has more tucked away than justified on a government salary, but as I said, he's a pretty successful gambler. That lines up with his mathematics background. And given that he's in WITSEC, he's pretty smart about it, accumulating some nice funds, but not too nice. Of course, who knows what else might be out there not linked in any way to this Goodman stuff?"

"Well, there's something here, given that we're not the only people looking."

"Agreed."

"Okay, I'm going to let Noack and Nguyen in on this. We're going to have to move quick to get to Clark."

"Paige, how is Jennifer?"

"Unfortunately, as far as I know, no change. Still in the coma, but she's hanging tough."

"Might not seem like it, but she's a tough lady."

"Yeah, Sean, I know."

"That's right, you do. And what about Stephen?"

Paige sighed. "He's where he should be – at her side. But if he gets wind of us moving to get Clark, I know he'll want to be in on it. So, we're not going to tell him, right?"

McEnany finished the last bit of water in the bottle. "Makes sense. Let the man be with his wife."

Chapter 47

"I don't like this flying by the seat of our pants crap," declared FBI Special Agent Rich Noack.

Trent Nguyen replied from the driver's seat of the Suburban, "We don't have much of a choice." Nguyen whipped the wheel to turn the vehicle across lanes and off of West Sahara Avenue.

He hit the brakes and pulled next to the Equinox parked at the curb.

Noack lowered his window. Charlie Driessen did the same in the Equinox.

Noack said, "I assume you're ready."

"Sure as hell," replied Driessen.

Caldwell nodded from the passenger seat as well.

Noack glanced into their back seat. "No Grant?"

"Doesn't know about this. He's with Jennifer," answered Caldwell.

"Good. Since there's no hiding at high noon, we move in fast. Fortunately, Goodman has no reason to expect us. Trent and I will enter from the front. You two cover the back. There will be no objections, so let's go."

The Suburban broke first, with the Equinox following. Nguyen made two turns and then a left onto Clark's street. He stopped the Suburban at the foot of the driveway where Clark's sedan was currently parked.

As Caldwell and Driessen moved into the backyard, Nguyen led the charge to the front door with his Glock 22 drawn. He paused, and looked through the glass door. He turned to Noack, who was just a step behind. "Inside door open."

Noack nodded. "Okay, move."

Nguyen opened the outside door, and announced, "This is the FBI. Mr. Goodman. FBI."

The living room was in a shambles. Two lamps were broken, a glass coffee table shattered, and the couch tipped over. A flat screen television also did not survive.

Nguyen declared, "Not good."

Caldwell and Driessen had entered from the kitchen door in the back of the house.

Moving from room to room, shouts of "Clear" were announced, until they made sure that no one was left in the house.

The four reconvened amidst the ruin of the living room. With a handgun hanging at her side, Caldwell looked around, and said, "Well, whoever the hell else was looking for Clark now has him."

Noack replied, "Would seem so. Crap." He pulled out his smartphone, and clicked twice. "West, somebody beat us to Clark."

Agent West asked, "You sure?"

Noack looked around the room, and said, "Yeah, we're pretty sure. You need to get a forensics team over here."

"Right away," she said. "Do you want me to contact the Marshal Service to check what they might know?"

Before Noack could reply, two men with guns drawn came through the front door, with "U.S. Marshal" scrolled in yellow across their dark blue bullet proof vests, followed by another three via the kitchen. The team leader screamed, "U.S. Marshals, drop your weapons, now!"

Caldwell actually raised her handgun in response.

But Nguyen quickly responded, "Relax, guys. We're FBI."

No one moved, while Noack spoke into his phone, "You know what, West, thanks anyway, but I can check with the Marshals myself."

Chapter 48

Everyone in the living room of Eric Clark's home eventually lowered their weapons, with Paige Caldwell the last to do so.

Then it was time for the two agencies' members to compare notes.

Caldwell went outside, and pulled out her phone.

Sean McEnany answered, "How'd it go?"

"We missed him. He was grabbed, and it's pretty clear that he didn't go willingly."

"I don't get it. I must be overlooking something."

"Talk to me," said Caldwell.

"There doesn't seem to be anything here. I've been digging on this guy. Called in a few favors to get better access, and nothing. Since his smuggling antiquities days, there's simply nothing to link him to any of this. And by the way, whoever did the cleaning on that antiquities business in Turkey, they did a pretty good job, but far from perfect."

"Yes, well, we obviously need better than pretty good," replied Caldwell offhandedly. "I'll talk with you later."

She ended the call with McEnany, and walked over to Driessen who was leaning on the Equinox watching the movement into and out of Clark's house. Caldwell positioned herself next to him. She whispered, "Sean's bewildered. He can't link Clark to any of this, in any way."

"What? Our man who mysteriously seems to know all doesn't actually know all. How can that possibly be?"

"Well, maybe it isn't possible, Charlie. There's always the chance that Sean does know all, and that there's actually not much to know about Mr. Donnie Goodman."

"Look at what's happening to this guy. Do you really think this is just a big screw-up?"

"Certainly wouldn't be the first."

"Yeah, but you're talking multiple screw-ups since we're obviously not the only ones interested."

Her eyes narrowed as she watched the house. "It doesn't have to be a screw-up necessarily."

"Oh, shit, come on."

Paige pulled her smartphone out and started strolling down the road.

Stephen answered on the first ring. "What's happening, Paige? I'm in the dark here." He whispered as he left Jennifer's side.

"You're not going to like it."

As he moved through the waiting room, Stephen signaled Ron, who nodded and moved to go in with Jennifer.

Stephen said, "What am I not going to like?"

He restrained himself from interrupting. While Paige gave a rundown on what they found out about Clark, and what happened at his house, Stephen's annoyance grew into anger. He could not get the picture of Jen beaten on the floor of the old house on the ranch out of his mind.

"Shit, Paige. Why didn't you let me know? I should have been in on that visit to Clark's."

"No, Stephen, you should have been where you are – with Jennifer."

"Don't tell me that. This is all about Jennifer, and I'm able to decide where I should be to help my wife best." The grip on his rage loosened just a hair.

"I know it's about Jennifer. I also know that you're not in the right place for making decisions about those who might or might not have been involved in hurting Jennifer."

Stephen continued to work on reining in his displeasure. "You know, you have a way of really pissing me off these days."

A faint, somewhat sad smile briefly crossed her mouth. Paige replied, "Yeah, I know. That actually hasn't changed over the years. I'll call you back when I know more."

Stephen began to reply, "You better, and ..." But Paige had already ended the call, which only got Stephen more aggravated.

God, help me get this under control.

Chapter 49

After glancing at the time in the upper right hand corner of the screen, Jonas Locke closed, unplugged, and sealed his laptop away in the safe in his home office.

He unlocked the door, stepped into the hallway, turned, and locked the door once again behind him with a key. Even the minimal noise his movements generated managed to launch his two children into action. They sprinted from the living room up the stairs, screeching all the way.

"Daddy, are we going to the game now?" asked his nine-year-old son, Terry.

"Yes, are we, are we?" added Jordan, a smiling seven-year-old girl.

"We sure are. It's a bit early, though, so how does lunch out somewhere sound, then we'll head over to the ballpark and watch our Giants kick some Padres butt?"

The two children laughed. Jordan said, "Daddy, you said butt." As their laughter grew, she added, "I'm telling, Mommy."

Jonas said, "You better not."

Terry announced, "We're both going to tell."

The two children raced down the stairs, and ran into the kitchen to tell their mother.

After hearing from her children, Peggy emerged from the kitchen as Jonas stepped off the stairs. She said, "Are you talking about people's butts again?"

This generated further laughter among the children.

"Guilty, as charged," he replied, and kissed his wife.

"Productive morning?" she asked.

"Very, and kind of interesting. It all took too long, but turned out to be a very lucrative few hours."

"Well, I like to hear that lucrative part."

Jordan walked by her parents to look out the front windows. "Daddy, I still can't see my bridge."

The Locke family lived in a two-story, cream-colored home, with terracotta roofing, across a narrow street from a lot where sightseers parked to visit the Golden Gate Bridge. On a clear day, the view of the bridge was breathtaking. But this was one of those days of dense fog, and only the base of the mighty structure could be seen.

Jordan put on a pouty face, and continued, "I hate when I can't see my bridge."

"I know, honey." Jonas moved next to her to look out the window. But it wasn't the bridge – or more precisely, its lack of visibility – that drew his attention.

A man in dark gray pants, shirt and hat, with long brown hair covering his neck, carrying a large toolbox, was moving away from the side of the house. He walked down the tiny lawn on a small hill, and across the road.

"Peg, who's the guy with the toolbox?"

She moved next to him. "Oh, I spoke to him a little while ago. He said he was with the cable company, checking some things out. They had gotten complaints that service was slow and spotty."

"Really?" As his wife went back to the kitchen, Jonas watched as the man popped the trunk on a white sedan, and dropped his equipment in, along with the hat. While glancing around, he also unbuttoned the gray shirt, tossed it in the trunk, pulled out a blue knit hat that he slipped on, and tucked his hair up underneath it. He now was dressed in a red t-shirt, a completely different hat, and appeared to have shorter hair. He closed the trunk, and got into the car.

Jonas observed, "That guy just changed his look, and is driving a car without any company markings." He paused, and then said, "Shit."

His daughter looked up. "What's wrong, Daddy?"

Jonas picked up his daughter, and grabbed his son's hand, dragging them both into the kitchen. "Peg, take the kids out back to the car."

She said, "What? What are you...?"

"Peg, just do it, right now. Could be nothing, but can't take any chances. Go! I've got to grab something from the office."

As he ran to the stairs, Peg called, "But Jonas..."

He screamed, "Get the hell out!"

As his family moved out the backdoor, Jonas struggled to get the office key out of his pocket. He finally did, and lunged across the room to the safe next to his desk.

But while he was struggling with the office door, the white sedan was pulling out of the parking lot. And just as Jonas placed his hand on the safe, the driver of the car pushed a key on his smartphone.

Jonas was able to only punch one number into the safe's keyboard when the house erupted in an explosion, transforming into a ball of intense fire.

Jonas' body was almost completely vaporized. Neighboring homes on each side of the Locke's house were partially ripped away.

Peg had just belted her children into the back seat, and taken a step back toward the house. She failed to survive the explosion.

The family car was thrown over and onto its roof by the blast. When they eventually began to recover from their burns and injuries days later, Terry and Jordan Locke would find themselves only with each other. An aunt and uncle would be left trying to fill the void of having lost their parents.

As the assassin drove on Lombard Street, he called the person who hired him. "It's done. Locke and his family are dead, and there's no way his computer survived the inferno."

"Good," said the voice on the other end of the call.

"Make sure the bonus is included. This was way too short notice. I don't do business like this. I've got to get out of this city, off the West Coast."

"Not yet. Lie low. I might have one more thing for you to do."

"Are you kidding?"

"No, I'm not fucking kidding."

"Okay, you'll pay for my time while I wait for you to make up your mind, and then whatever else you've got will be another bonus job. Got it?"

"No problem."

The assassin turned out not only to be wrong about the entire family being dead, but about Jonas' laptop as well.

Chapter 50

It wasn't the terrorist attacks on September 11, 2001, that led Sean McEnany to redirect what he was doing with his life.

McEnany's epiphany had come three years earlier.

He had been an Army Ranger for a few years when two U.S. embassies – one in Nairobi, Kenya, and the other in Dar es Salaam, Tanzania – were bombed, resulting in the deaths of 234 people, including 12 Americans, and more than 4,600 being injured.

McEnany made his frustrations clear to superiors regarding the U.S. response, or as McEnany put it, "Our pathetic lack of response to a growing terrorist threat." They listened to and were impressed by McEnany's analysis of what it would take to fight "a war that's already been declared on us."

McEnany excelled far beyond even his elite fellow Rangers in all areas of expertise, but especially in intelligence gathering, and insertions demanding that the enemy be surprised and shocked.

Therefore, the soldiers that McEnany worked with were surprised and shocked when he announced his decision to leave the Army, and go to work for a private security firm.

CorpSecQuest, and its subsidiary GovSecQuest, however, added up to anything but a straightforward private security business. The firm certainly gave every outward appearance of being a legitimate business, with a wide array of real contracts, actual work, and notable revenues and profits. However, a handful of personnel had ties with key government intelligence services, and those ties were so deeply buried that only an elite few inside government and inside the firm itself had knowledge of the assorted undertakings on behalf of national security.

During his interviews with the founders of CorpSecQuest, McEnany emphasized his desire to work on varying fronts in the war against global terrorists.

By the time the U.S. got hit on 9-11, Sean McEnany had been at CorpSecQuest for nearly a year and a half, and was completing graduate degrees in both computer science and international business. Not long thereafter, he had risen to become the most valuable employee in the company, given his Ranger training, technological expertise, and contacts seemingly everywhere on the globe. Yet, most people he worked with thought he was merely another GovSecQuest vice president who groomed and maintained good contacts on Capitol Hill and at the Pentagon, while sometimes drumming up business internationally as well.

To his fellow office dwellers, McEnany appeared to be an adequate, workmanlike cog in the firm's wheels. But to those in the shadows who actually ran the enterprise, Sean McEnany was a valued, lethal secret weapon.

Even when McEnany's wife started pushing to move out of Washington, D.C., and back to Long Island where she grew up, it turned out to be an opportunity for McEnany. Under the guise of telecommuting from a home office, he gained even greater freedom to do the work for which the firm had been set up.

After arriving on Long Island, McEnany's CIA contact – Tank Hoard – suggested that, if looking for a nice church for the family, Sean might want to consider St. Mary's Lutheran Church in Manorville, which just happened to be led by a former agency operative. So, the McEnany family dropped their Methodism in favor of Lutheranism, with Sean rather quickly joining the church council.

Pastor Stephen Grant was glad to have McEnany around for church matters, and for other non-church challenges that eventually cropped up.

Hoard was pleased to keep two former CIA operatives – Paige Caldwell and Charlie Driessen – in his orbit by having them work with McEnany.

Sean further expanded his reach and abilities to execute his own personal war on terrorists, and all others who threatened his country, its citizens, and their allies.

Chapter 51

An hour after the home explosion in San Francisco, Sean McEnany received word that Jonas Locke and his wife were dead.

His first call was home. Without revealing what happened, Sean spoke caringly with his wife, Rachel, and each of their three children.

Before hanging up, Sean told his wife, "You know, honey, I'm not sure yet, but I might have to fly out to California – the San Francisco area – for a quick meeting when I'm done with the current assignment."

They spoke a bit more about travel plans, and before ending the call, Sean said, "I love you."

McEnany's next call was to Paige Caldwell. He informed her, "My source on Clark, Jonas Locke, is dead."

"What?"

"His home was blown sky high. His wife is dead, too. The two young kids were hurt, but they'll make it – well, as far as they can without their parents."

"I trust there was no way anyone could have known that he was working with you?"

"I took precautions in our dealings, and Jonas was careful," answered McEnany, with his annoyance clear. "We find whoever else got the information on Clark, and we find the bastards who did this."

"I know."

"First Jennifer, and now Jonas is dead. I want these guys bad."

"So do I, Sean. Believe me."

"The house bombing was meant for more than just taking out my colleague. It had a high burn factor, meant to incinerate more than just bodies. This was designed to eliminate everything, including any trace of links to Jonas."

Caldwell asked, "Did they succeed in wiping out all of the information?"

"That I don't know. But I've got someone on site from San Francisco P.D. picking through what's left."

Chapter 52

Dixon Shaw made a right off of North Las Vegas Blvd., then another right and a left into a driveway in the opening of a six-foot wall. He parked his Ferrari next to a black van.

Shaw got out of the car. He paused to look at the walls on each side of the parking lot, and then at the slightly rundown, beige building.

He took a deep breath, and entered.

Waiting at a cheap, pressed-wood desk were Two Gloves Geraci and his assistant.

"Where's this Clark, or Donnie Goodman?" Shaw demanded.

Geraci said, "In the back room. I've got everything ready."

Shaw glanced at Geraci's assistant, who was sporting a black eye. Dix said to Geraci, "Apparently, he didn't come easily."

"He came, eventually."

"I don't want to waste time arguing with this prick. Two Gloves, are you sure he did this?"

"Well, Chet is. The stuff Gino gave you lines up with what Chet found. Said he compared, checked and rechecked everything, and you know how thorough he is. It's all there, Dix." Geraci pointed his right, gloved index finger at a file on top of the desk.

Shaw picked the file up, opened it, and started flipping through the assorted pages.

As Shaw read, Geraci continued, "You'll see money transfers, cellphone records, and even the transaction information and title showing that Goodman bought the ranch where Gil Rice held Jennifer. With Chet and Gino on the same page, no doubt this is the fucking guy behind Jennifer's kidnapping."

"Son of a bitch. And he's not trying to get at me?"

"The history is in the file as well. It goes back to your son-in-law. At the CIA, Grant nailed Goodman for running a smuggling operation. Looks like this guy stewed for a hell of a long time, and then saw his opportunity."

"But how could he have known that Jennifer and Grant would be coming here?"

"Yeah, I wondered that myself, and asked Chet. If you look at the stuff about the conference Jennifer spoke at, the dates line up pretty nice."

"What do you mean?" replied Shaw, flipping between pages.

"A couple of days after it was announced that Jennifer would be a speaker at the conference, you can see Goodman kicking into action. He got wind of Jennifer coming, found out or knew who she was married to, and got his fucking plan rolling."

Shaw closed the file, and placed it back on the desk. He said, "Stay here."

He stepped around the desk, moved deliberately to the door leading to the back room, turned the gold-colored knob, and stepped inside.

Eric Clark was lying on a large, plastic tarp, which would make for easy clean up and disposal. His hands and legs were bound, and mouth taped.

Shaw picked up a handgun that was waiting for him on the lone table in the room. He walked over, squatted in front of Clark, and poked the prisoner in the head as he made his points. "Mr. Goodman, or Mr. Clark, you chose to take your revenge out on the wrong woman."

Clark worked to talk despite the tape, while shaking his head.

Shaw continued to poke Clark. "Stop, stop," he said with a calmness in his voice. "It's not going to do you any good. You hired, or worked with Mr. Rice, however you want to put it. He has been eliminated, not by me, but that's okay, as long as the job gets done. And now you will be taken care of."

Clark struggled against his bindings, and started shaking his head once more.

Shaw looked up and down Clark's body. "My daughter was bound by Rice, similar to the way you are right now, I believe. Rice, though, was a fucking head case. He had real issues, and beat my daughter to near death. In fact, I'm still not sure she's going to make it."

Shaw dropped from the squat onto his knees. He leaned down, moving his face within a few inches of Clark's. "I'm a better man than Rice, however, and you should be thankful. I'm not going to beat you to death. I'm a businessman. As you can tell" – he pointed at the tarp spread out on the floor – "I don't like when things get messy. Like I said, get the job done."

Shaw then stood up. "So, I'm going to get the job done efficiently by putting a much-deserved bullet in your brain."

He pointed the gun, and pulled the trigger. And then he fired two more shots. "Well, maybe three shots in your brain."

Shaw put the gun back on the table, and left the room.

As he walked toward the front door, Shaw said, "Nice job, Nicky. Thank Chet for me. Please make sure everything is cleaned up. I've got to get back to the hospital."

Geraci said, "Of course, Dix."

Chapter 53

Rich Noack quickly drained his third bottle of cold water in just over an hour, and wiped sweat off his forehead. "Okay, so let's sum up."

He was standing with Agents Nguyen and West outside the home of the onetime Eric Clark at the back of an FBI evidence truck. It was nearly three-and-a-half hours since they first arrived to find the house turned upside down, and no sign of Clark.

Nguyen said, "We've got nothing from the house indicating that Clark was involved with the kidnapping of Jennifer Grant. The Marshals have nothing either. They said Clark's life as Donnie Goodman has been downright boring. His main interest is playing relatively small stakes poker at assorted casinos around town. They said he is good at it, but makes sure not to be crazy good. He's pretty careful. In fact, when he almost sat down at a poker table with Grant on Wednesday, Goodman called WITSEC."

"What about a link to Dixon Shaw?"

Nguyen replied, "Nothing that the Marshals could point to."

West added, "That all lines up with what we've found – or haven't found – on Clark, given his phone, online, financial activities, and so on."

Noack replied, "Okay, where the hell is he then? Why is his house ripped apart?" He grunted. "Go over it all again.

We've got to be missing something." Noack looked at Nguyen, "I'm going to call Caldwell and see if McEnany has anything else."

"If anyone is able to get information we can't, I'd bet on McEnany."

"Makes you wonder what he's really about. How the hell does he get at stuff that we, the FBI, can't? He's just a private contractor."

Nguyen smiled. "Maybe he's not *just* a contractor. Never know."

"Yeah, thanks." Noack hit "Paige Caldwell" on his smartphone's contact list.

She answered, "Noack, what do you have?"

"Nothing, that's the problem. We haven't found anything yet linking Clark to any of this. Maybe he's just that good, and we're not there yet. But I wanted to see if your business partner, Mr. McEnany, might be able to dig anything up. He does seem to have rather unique contacts or means of getting information, if I recall."

"He not only hasn't found anything, but one of his key sources on Clark was just killed in a house explosion in San Francisco."

"Shit. Somebody's cleaning things up, and we've got to figure who the hell it is before the work is done."

Chapter 54

After Paige hung up with Noack, she looked at Charlie Driessen, who was clicking away on a laptop with his two index fingers. Paige and Charlie had returned a couple of hours earlier to Driessen's hotel room, which now served as their base of operations.

Driessen said, "Still nothing from the feds?"

"Worse than nothing. No one can link any of this to Clark."

"Maybe your hunch was right. Clark was set up as the fall guy, and all evidence is being erased?"

"Maybe. Let's hope the erasers haven't made everything disappear." She took a breath. "I'm calling Stephen. It's time that he finds out everything Dixon Shaw knows."

* * *

Stephen asked, "Sean doesn't have anything interesting yet on Dix?"

Paige said, "Well, there's some interesting stuff, more than a few accusations regarding hardball business tactics, as well as rumors going back on some rather old-school mob strong-arming. But at this point, nothing earth-shattering."

"Okay, Paige. You're right. It's time to get more out of my father-in-law directly." He ended the call.

Would it really surprise me to learn that Dix had Oliver Rice offed? Already know he compartmentalizes. But what about who's behind this, and what's going on with the cleanup operation?

Stephen returned from the hallway to Jennifer's room. Ron looked up from a bedside chair. He blessed himself, rose, dropped rosary beads in his pocket, and gave Stephen a pat on the shoulder as he went to leave.

Stephen glanced at his watch. Nearly 4:30 PM. He said to Ron, "Can you hang around?"

"Of course."

"I'll be out in a couple of minutes. Maybe Joan can come in then."

Ron looked Stephen in the eyes. "I'm sure she will. What is it?"

"I've got something to do when Dix returns."

Ron hesitated, and then said, "I'll be in the waiting room."

Stephen moved to Jennifer's side. He gently ran his hand over her hair, longing to see her beautiful brown eyes open, once again bright with life. It was the sound of the respirator that ramped up the knot in his stomach and ache in his chest. He said another prayer pleading for his wife's healing, and then leaned down to gently kiss her hand.

Stephen stared at Jennifer's face, waiting for some kind of signal. He got none, and left.

As he walked toward the waiting room, Grant worked on transforming his aching for Jennifer into a steely determination to get the answers he needed from her father.

Dix had returned, and was in the waiting room with Ron and Joan. "How is she, Pastor?"

"The same," Stephen replied coolly.

Dix started to move past Stephen, saying, "I need to see her."

Stephen, however, raised his arm, and placed his hand on Dix's chest. "Not yet, if you don't mind. Why don't we let Joan go in with Jen? Then we can talk for a few minutes."

As Stephen and Dix stared at each other, with Grant's hand still on Shaw's chest, Ron said, "Would you mind going in with Jennifer for a while, Joan?"

Joan's eyes were transfixed on Stephen and Dix. When she looked at Ron, he tilted his head in the direction of Jennifer's room. Joan managed a smile. "Mind? Um, of course not. I'll go in right now."

As Joan left, Stephen finally lowered his arm, and Dix replied, "Sure, Pastor, let's talk."

Stephen replied, "Not here. We'll go for a walk."

Grant left the room, and Shaw followed. They rode the elevator and walked through the hospital lobby in silence.

When they exited the front doors, Shaw finally said, "All right, Pastor, what is it?"

Stephen continued to move away from the traffic of the hospital entrance. He turned the corner of the building and moved into a short alleyway between the hospital building and parking garage.

Apparently having enough of the silence and the walk, Shaw reached out and put his hand on Grant's shoulder, beginning, "What the...?"

Before another word was uttered, Stephen grabbed Dix's arm, pulled his father-in-law forward, and with his free hand, pushed Shaw face-first into the brick wall.

Dix said, "What the fuck are you doing? Have you lost it?"

Dix struggled to get free, but Stephen was unrelenting. With arm turned and pinned against his back, Shaw could not move, not, that is, without generating pain.

Grant whispered in Shaw's ear. "Listen, Dix, it's time for you to come clean. I need to know everything. Why did Gil Rice say that you killed his son?"

"I told you that I don't know..."

Grant pushed Shaw's arm up higher.

Shaw grunted in pain. "Shit, stop it. I mean it on Rice."

Stephen replied, "Why don't I believe you?" He eased off a hair on Shaw. "Somehow, you're at the center of this entire thing, Dix."

"Me? I don't think so, Pastor."

"What do you mean?"

"Look at yourself. You mentioned a man named Eric Clark. He's from your history, not mine." Shaw failed to hide the anger in his voice.

Grant released the arm, turned Shaw around, and used his forearm to exert pressure on his father-in-law's neck. "What the hell do you mean? I thought you said you didn't know who Clark was?"

"I didn't. But I'm a man of means, Pastor. I'm not going to sit still when my daughter's kidnapped. I want all the people involved to pay. And I got information on your background with Eric Clark."

Grant pulled his arm off Shaw, and took a small step back. The older man quickly clenched his right fist, drew it back, and began to move it at Grant's face. But even given his many years away from the CIA and SEALs, Grant's instincts were sharp, at least sharp enough to deal with Shaw. Grant leaned back and to the side. After Shaw's punch missed its mark, Stephen reacted with a quick left into Dix's ribs, and then a right elbow to the side of the face.

Grant held back on the severity of each blow, but Shaw nonetheless toppled to the cement. *Well, there goes any chance for future Thanksgiving dinners.*

Shaw grimaced, and shifted up onto his hands and knees. "I'm starting not to like you, Pastor." He then gradually got to his feet, and looked Grant in the eyes. "Yes, I know what happened with the smuggling operation, and your role in getting Clark pushed out of the CIA. Sounds like motive to me."

Grant sighed, and decided to give Dix some added information. "Yes, well, it sounded like motive to others as well. But it's been checked out. Clark wasn't involved."

"That's not what I heard."

"What the hell does that mean?"

"Information has been provided that Clark was very much involved." Without giving away too much, Shaw summarized some of the information that was supplied to him. He concluded, "It was all there, clear ... and actionable." Shaw then smiled slightly.

"Actionable? What did you do, Dix?"

"I have not done anything that a father should not do."

Oh, no.

Grant said, "Nobody can find Eric Clark. Do you know where he is?"

"Of course not, Pastor."

"Well, I hope not because your information is wrong. Some of the best sources on the planet can't find a link. In fact, things might point to Clark being a fall guy, a patsy." Grant filled Shaw in just enough.

Stephen watched his father-in-law's poker face drop.

"That's impossible," Dix declared. "It doesn't make any sense." Shaw started walking back and forth in the alley, his right hand rubbing his chin. "How could that be?"

You idiot. You've done something to Clark. Stephen asked slowly, "Dix, you grabbed Clark, didn't you? What did you have done to him? Where is he?"

Stephen could see Dix's mind working, distant from their conversation. He grabbed Shaw's shoulder. "Dix, what's going on?"

Shaw pulled away, and said, "You know what, Pastor? I don't know what's going on. But I'm sure as shit going to find out." He turned and started walking away.

Grant said, "Dix, where the hell are you going?"

Shaw said over his shoulder, "Got to get some answers. We'll talk later."

After Shaw disappeared around the corner, Grant pulled his BlackBerry out, and dialed Paige. When she answered, Stephen announced, "This just keeps getting better by the minute."

"What now?" Paige replied.

"Can't be 100 percent sure, call it one of my gut feelings, but I think my father-in-law had Eric Clark killed."

Chapter 55

Dixon Shaw blew out of the elevator and past the secretary sitting outside Nicky Geraci's office.

"Good afternoon, Mr. Shaw," she said.

Without even a glance, Shaw said, "Go home, Marla, now."

He entered Geraci's office without knocking, slammed the door shut, and moved to the desk where Two Gloves sat.

Geraci said, "Dix, what's up?"

Shaw placed his hands on the desktop. "What the fuck did you do, Nicky?"

Geraci leaned backed slightly in his chair. "What are you talking about?"

"Grant tells me that Eric Clark had nothing to do with Jennifer's kidnapping."

Geraci pushed his chair back. "Dix, that's impossible. You saw the information. They've got to be wrong."

"Yeah, well, apparently the massive resources of the FBI and CIA, and who knows what else, cannot find any links between Clark and Rice." He raised his voice. "In fact, they think Clark was a fucking patsy, set up to take the fall."

"How the hell could that be?" Geraci ran a gloved hand through his thick hair. "The feds must have missed the information we got."

"Really? That's what you're going with? The feds somehow missed all of that information. Are you kidding?" Geraci moved across the room to a small bar, poured a bourbon, and downed it in one gulp. "I don't know, Dix."

Shaw walked over and stopped in front of Geraci. Their faces were less than a foot apart. "It's getting clearer to me, Two Gloves. Somebody gave us bad information." Shaw's eyes bore in on Geraci's.

Two Gloves slammed the glass down on the bar counter, and actually moved his face even closer to Dix's. "Are you accusing me, old friend?"

Dix said nothing, simply staring, unblinking at Geraci.

Two Gloves continued, "No answer? You shit. And you're supposed to be the brains, and me the muscle."

Geraci stepped back and poured two more drinks. He handed one to Dix, grabbed the second glass, and moved back to his desk.

Shaw said, "What are you talking about?"

Geraci sat in his chair, and only took a sip of the bourbon this time. "There are only two possibilities, right? First, the feds are wrong, and apparently you've ruled that out. If that's the case, then the question is: Who provided the bad info?"

Dix said, "We had two sources."

"Right, two sources – Chet and Gino."

"Chet?"

"Why not? You just thought it was me, didn't you? Why not Chet?"

Shaw downed the bourbon. "Chet and Gino have worked together before on a few projects."

"Yeah, they have."

"But why?"

"Shit, I don't know."

An unmistakable anger entered Shaw's voice. "Find out. No more mistakes. No more being played. Get it right. And then, if Chet was in on this, he's a dead man."

"I'm on it." As Shaw turned and left the office, Two Gloves drank the remainder of his bourbon, put the glass down and tugged on his black gloves.

Chapter 56

As Dixon Shaw drove off to meet with Geraci, Grant went back into the hospital.

Stephen entered the waiting room with strain and distraction on his face.

Ron took one look at his friend, and asked, "You okay?"

Grant sighed, sat down and placed his face in his hands, with elbows resting on his knees. After a moment, he dropped his hands, and leaned back in the chair. "I don't know the answer to that question, Ron."

"What happened?"

"Well..." Stephen paused. *How much do I tell him?* Grant decided that he needed to talk. "I had a confrontation with my father-in-law."

On the outside, Ron took that smoothly. "From what I saw, that confrontation started in this room."

"It grew then into an altercation outside."

"And what exactly does that mean?"

"It's pretty clear that Gil Rice and his accomplices at the ranch were not working by themselves. We're trying to figure out who else was behind Jen's kidnapping."

"And your father-in-law?"

"There's some reason to think that what happened to Jen might be somehow tied to getting at Dix. Perhaps revenge." *Not too far, Grant.* "He has a colorful background in a tough, some might say sordid, business."

Ron had been pacing slowly, and then sat down next to Stephen. "And what did your father-in-law tell you?"

Definitely cannot go there. "It only seemed to raise more questions."

"Was this definitely linked to Shaw?"

"Definite? No. Like I said, more questions."

"Well, I'm sure you've thought of this, Stephen, but what about your background? You know, with the CIA. Could someone behind this be trying to get back at you? Or have I just read too many crazy thrillers?"

Grant managed a small chuckle. He looked at his friend. "No, you haven't read too many spy novels. That's a possibility. In fact, you apparently think like my father-in-law. He asked the same question."

Before Ron could respond, the door swung open, and Joan said, "Stephen, please come in. The doctor wants you."

Grant's heart rate accelerated as he jumped to his feet, passed through the door, and moved to Jennifer's side. Joan and Ron waited just outside the doorway to Jennifer's room.

Stephen looked at his wife's still closed eyes, and then turned his focus to Dr. Harper on the other side of the bed.

Harper said, "Jennifer has gotten a bit stronger. Her vitals have improved and grown steadier, which is a good sign. So, I'd like to take her off the ventilator."

Stephen felt a different kind of excitement for the first time in quite a while. There was a hopeful jump in his heart. *God, thank you.* He whispered, "Of course."

Harper added, "Stephen, your wife is still in a delicate place. We obviously have to continue to watch her closely. My hope is that this improvement will translate into consciousness at some point soon. But unfortunately, I can't be specific on what 'soon' actually means."

Stephen gently covered Jennifer's hand with his own, and said, "I understand. Thanks so much for what you and your staff have done, Dr. Harper."

"Of course, Pastor Grant. And by the way, I happen to think that prayer helps as well."

The two men smiled at each other as Harper left the room.

Chapter 57

Following the Saturday night service at St. Mary's Lutheran Church, Zack squeezed two additional chairs into his office so Beatrice Aiken could be joined by her parents.

After going over the final details of Jay's viewing and funeral, Beatrice and her parents fell into an uncomfortable silence.

Zack asked, "Is there anything else?"

Beatrice's mother held her daughter's hand, but neither parent looked at Zack or Beatrice.

Beatrice finally replied, "Why do people have to be so difficult at the worst possible times?"

Zack said, "There are lots of answers to that question. What's going on?"

The parents still did not look up.

Beatrice bit her lower lip, as her eyes welled up. "They just have to make it about themselves." She took a deep breath. "Blair and I argued some more over the psychic stuff. Now she says she's not coming to the funeral here at the church, and won't stay in the room during the wake when we pray."

"I see," replied Zack.

Beatrice's father finally looked at Charmichael. "We're not very proud of Blair, Pastor."

"Not very proud? She's being a jackass," declared Beatrice. Hurt was now being mixed with anger in her voice and expression. "And then Jay's parents made a big stink about the funeral being here, in his own church, and him being buried near his own home. They wanted to take him, take my husband, back to Oklahoma. What's wrong with people, Pastor? Why are they doing this?" She broke down, turned and cried into her mother's shoulder.

"I'm so sorry, Bee," said Zack. "People don't think sometimes. Jay's parents lost their son, so they're in pain just like you. I can understand their impulse. Right?"

In exasperation, Beatrice replied, "I guess."

"But they also need to understand that Jay started his own family."

"Yes, he did," she replied in a weak voice.

"Are they all right with things now?"

Beatrice half shrugged. "I think so. They said they are, and even apologized. I know that should be enough, but I'm just so frustrated."

The four fell silent.

Beatrice's mother asked, "Can we say a prayer, for Jay as well, Pastor?"

"Well, if you'd like to, that's fine. But Jay's not the one in need of prayer today. He's with Jesus. It's the rest of us who are struggling with his loss. The rest of us need to be healed. We need solace from the Great Comforter. We can't let Jay's loss lead us to a dark place where we lose sight of the love and strength that come from our Savior."

The four bowed their heads.

Chapter 58

It was 9:30 at night, less than three hours since Shaw had left Geraci's office. But now Two Gloves sat across from Dix in the office of the Casino Beach penthouse.

Geraci said, "Chet approached Gino. Then they hired Gil Rice. But Rice went too far by grabbing Jen. She wasn't supposed to be part of the plan."

Dix clenched his fists. "What plan?"

"You were the target, Dix. Apparently, our old buddy, Chet, wants you dead."

"How the hell do you know this, Nicky?"

Geraci smirked. "Because Gino told me."

"And why did he do that?"

"I gave him no other option."

Shaw picked up a crystal globe paperweight off his desk. He got up and started walking around the office, tossing the globe up in the air and catching it. "And did Gino say why Chet wants to put me six feet under?"

Geraci shook his head. "Said he had no clue. All he knew was that Chet promised a huge payday not too far down the road."

"Well, with me dead, Chet would get a bigger chunk of the casinos."

"Yes, he would."

"And what about you?"

"Yeah, I kind of wondered about that myself. Gino claimed that I never came up."

"Do you believe him?"

"I used the carrot and the stick. Seems like he was being straight."

Dix stopped tossing the crystal globe in the air. Instead, his knuckles turned white as he tightened his grip on it. "Is Gino dead?"

"No. I figured that's your decision, Dix. But he ain't talking to anybody right now."

A few moments of silence passed, and then Geraci asked, "What do you want to do about Chet?"

"What do I want to do?" hissed Dix. He turned and hurled the crystal globe at a glass section of the office wall. The wall spider-webbed, and then shattered. Shards of glass of varying shapes and sizes crashed to the floor.

The noise generated a response from Candy, who came from the bedroom in a pink negligee and bare feet. "Oh, my God. Dix, what happened?"

Dix looked at her through the open space where the wall once was. "A misunderstanding, Candy. Don't worry. Go back to our bedroom."

"But Dix, this..."

Shaw raised his voice. "Candy, stop. I've got bigger things to worry about. Go back inside. When Nicky and I go out, I'll send someone up to clean this up."

She turned and left.

Nicky asked, "Are we going out?"

"Well, we've got to get to Chet before he realizes that Gino isn't reachable."

"Right. As far as I know, he's at home."

"The little bastard, our supposed friend, has to pay the price, and his body has to disappear."

"What are you thinking?"

Shaw resumed his pacing around the office, with his black shoes crunching on broken glass. "Old school."

Geraci leaned back in his chair. "I'm listening."

"They're still pouring concrete at The River. Everything we need is right there."

"That is old school. I like it." He clapped his gloved hands, and rubbed them together. "I'll call my assistant and have him clear out the security guard, turn off the cameras, and make sure we've got the mixture ready."

Shaw asked, "Good. Can we get Chet out of his house without anyone knowing it?"

"Easier than you think. We'll leave here quietly. When we get to Chet's, I should be able to get him out the door without too much trouble. I'll blame one of your late night creative moments, and that we need to go to the site to explore some new ideas. And I don't think he and Angelica have slept in the same bed for months."

"Creative moments?"

"That's what I call it when you want to talk about big projects in the middle of the night. It's not like you haven't gotten us together before in the middle of the night."

Dix walked through the now-nonexistent office wall, across the hallway, and picked up the still intact crystal ball. He returned the sphere to his desk, and said, "Nothing creative tonight, Nicky. Just a bullet to the head, and Chet's body encased in concrete."

Chapter 59

Sean McEnany ignored the luminous moon outside the window. His attention had not wavered from the glow of two computer screens for several hours.

He stopped scrolling through spreadsheets on each screen, and looked from one screen to the other – back and forth.

McEnany whispered to himself, "Holy crap. Thanks for being so damn thorough, Jonas."

He grabbed the smartphone resting on the table, and called Paige Caldwell.

She answered, "Sean, what do you have?"

"Thankfully, Jonas was careful and meticulous. The blast didn't destroy his laptop. It was tucked away in a safe that could nearly survive a nuclear blast. I helped my S.F.P.D. person gain access to the hard drive, and upload the contents to my cloud space, and ever since, I've been cracking open the files. Jonas had tight security, but he had even tighter recordkeeping."

"That's great, Sean, but less process. What's the bottom line?"

"Two things. First, Dixon Shaw's partner, Chet Easton, is the moneyman. It's clear that he was the one paying Jonas for the WITSEC information about Clark."

"Son of a bitch. This is about some kind of battle between Dixon Shaw and Chet Easton. Thanks, Sean. That's critical."

"Wait. I said there were two items on this bottom line."

"Okay, number two?"

"Jonas's records show that it's not just Easton. While Easton took care of the payments, it was the other partner, Geraci, who gave the work to Jonas in the first place."

"You've got to be kidding me – both of Shaw's partners were in on framing Eric Clark for having Jennifer kidnapped and beaten. What the hell is this about?"

Sean replied, "Shaw's partners are out to hurt him. For some reason, getting at Jennifer was part of this plan. But now things are being cleaned up, and I would assume, finished up. And that means..."

Paige finished his sentence, "... Dixon Shaw has to be cleaned up."

"Right."

"Thanks, Sean." Paige ended the call.

Sean said, "You're welcome," to no one. He refocused on the computer terminals. "And now, I need a bit more information from Mr. Easton and Mr. Geraci."

Chapter 60

Stephen sat next to Jennifer's bed with his eyes closed. He wasn't sleeping, but was trying to quietly regain some strength, as he had learned to do as a SEAL.

The phone rumbled in his pocket. He pulled it out, and saw Paige's name. *Please have something.* "Hi, Paige. Anything?"

"Yes, unfortunately. Is Shaw with you?"

Stephen knew the tone and intensity in Paige's voice all too well. He rose from the chair, and headed out of Jennifer's room. "He's not. Why?"

There was no one in the waiting room, as Stephen insisted that Joan and Ron head back to their rooms at The Twenties for a full night's sleep.

"Where is he?"

"As far as I know, he's at the Casino Beach. What's happening?"

"Stephen, both his partners, Easton and Geraci, were in on framing Clark, and had their hands in Jennifer's kidnapping."

"Are you sure?" Grant knew he didn't need to ask, but reflexively did anyway.

"Sean's got it all. They had Sean's contact killed as well."

Grant was ahead in the calculations. "And this is all about getting at Dix. He's the target, and it's time to clean everything up."

"Looks like it."

"I'm at the hospital."

"We're set up in Charlie's room at Casino Beach."

"Get upstairs to the penthouse. I'm thinking that's where Dix should be."

"We're on it. Back to you shortly."

Chapter 61

The elevator doors opened on the top floor of the Casino Beach Vegas Resort. Paige Caldwell and Charlie Driessen stepped into the spacious vestibule and pulled out their handguns.

Paige hit the penthouse's buzzer, and banged on the door.

No answer.

She repeated the same process, this time ringing the buzzer three times, and banging louder and longer.

Driessen checked the doorknob, which was locked. He shrugged, "Hey, you never know." He looked up and down the door. "We're not kicking this in."

Paige said, "You're right. Step back."

"Oh, come on, you're not."

"No time."

Paige pointed the Glock, and chewed up the doorknob and lock with seven shots.

"So much for the element of surprise," Driessen observed.

Caldwell led the way, now easily pushing the door open. She shouted, "Dixon Shaw! Shaw, are you here?"

There were no sounds.

Caldwell and Driessen began sweeping through the massive apartment when Charlie came across the shattered glass. "Paige, check this out."

She moved in from the kitchen, and surveyed the scene.

The two proceeded to move through the penthouse.

When Driessen opened a bedroom door, a cry came from Candy Welles, who was hiding next to the bed hugging a pillow. "Please, please, don't shoot me."

"Crap, I'm not going to shoot you. We're here to help. Why didn't you answer the door?"

Candy struggled to get her breathing under control. "Who are you?"

"Friends of Stephen Grant."

She seemed perplexed by the answer, but managed to say, "I-I was listening to music, but then I heard shots."

Paige entered the room. "We need to know where Dixon is."

"Dix? He only left a few minutes ago. He went with Nicky."

Caldwell and Driessen glanced at each other.

Paige asked, "What happened with the shattered glass?"

Candy said, "Um, I'm not really sure. I think Dix got mad."

Driessen observed, "Apparently. Where are Shaw and Geraci now?"

Candy continued, "I don't know where they went. Is Dix all right? What's wrong?"

Paige replied, "We have to find him to make sure he is okay. Can you call him?"

"What? Yes, yes." She picked up the phone on the nightstand.

The sound of Dean Martin singing "Ain't That a Kick in the Head" came from outside the bedroom.

Candy said, "That's our ringtone. He left his phone here."

Driessen said, "Oh, great."

Caldwell looked at Candy. "Ms. Welles, security is going to be up here any second. Can you make sure that we get out of here quickly to help Dixon?"

"To help, Dix? Of course." She dropped the pillow, got to her feet, and walked out of the bedroom in her pink negligee.

Driessen's eyes followed Candy's long legs.

Paige said to him, "Eyes up, soldier."

"Only human, Paige."

Voices of the Casino Beach security personnel called out, "Mr. Shaw, Ms. Welles, are you okay?"

With as much authority as a beautiful woman could muster standing in skimpy, pink nightwear, Candy Welles got Paige and Charlie out the door in less than three minutes.

Heading down the elevator, Paige called Stephen and relayed what had happened in the penthouse.

Stephen said, "Can you two get over here to pick me up?"

Paige said, "We'll be there in five or so."

Chapter 62

Grant hung up with Ron McDermott, who promised to be over to the hospital as quick as he could.

Who can I call on this? He held out little hope, but nonetheless called the offices of Easton and Geraci. Each went to voice mail.

What now? He remembered how helpful Lou Hammett, executive director of The Twenties, had been on the tour of the resort when they first arrived. He glanced at the time on his phone. *It's Vegas, so 10:30 is early in the night.*

Grant was immediately transferred to Hammett's line. "What can I do for you, Pastor Grant?"

"Mr. Hammett, this is an emergency, and I think you're the only one who can help."

"Of course, what is it?"

"Your boss may be in trouble, and I need to find him."

"Dix?"

"Yes, and he doesn't have his phone with him. I need cell numbers for Chet Easton and Nicky Geraci." It occurred to Grant that he had no pen or paper, so he moved to the nurse's desk, and made a silent plea for writing utensils.

Hammett gave Grant each number, and then asked, "Do you want their home numbers as well?"

"Yes, thanks."

Again, Grant's limited hopes were dashed as each call to cells went directly to voice mail.

Then the home line of Nicky Geraci just kept ringing. He finally called Chet Easton's home. To his surprise, a woman answered, "Hello."

Grant recognized the voice of Angelica Easton. "Mrs. Easton, this is Pastor Stephen Grant. We met at dinner the other night."

"Pastor...? Right, you're married to Dix's daughter." She barely hid her irritation. "What do you want?"

"Well, I'm at the hospital and trying to track down my father-in-law."

"The hospital?" Her tone softened a bit, as Stephen hoped it would. "Oh, that's right. How is your wife?"

"She seems to be getting stronger. Thank you. Like I said, I'm trying to get a hold of Dix, and..."

"Yeah, sure. Chet just left here like five minutes ago with Nicky. They told me they were meeting with Dix to work through some plans."

As he spoke to Angelica, Paige and Charlie emerged through the doors of ICU. Stephen nodded at them, as he asked Angelica, "Do you know where they were going?"

Her irritation returned. "That little shit, Chet, doesn't tell me much. They said they were just going to a meeting, but I overheard them. They were going with Dix to The River site."

"Thank you so much, Mrs. Easton." Grant hung up, and turned to Paige and Charlie. "Geraci and Easton are with Dix. According to Easton's wife, they're on the way to the construction site for Dix's next casino. We've got to get to them, now."

Paige said, "Let's go."

Grant took a step, and then stopped. "Charlie, can you stay with Jennifer?"

Driessen said, "What?"

"Ron McDermott is on the way, but I can't leave her alone. And I can't be sure if she's safe with everything going on."

Driessen began, "Then why don't you stay, and..." The look from Paige stopped Charlie's protest. He continued, "Shit, fine. Go, I've got this covered."

Stephen said, "Thanks, Charlie."

Driessen grunted something in response.

Grant and Caldwell exited the ICU.

Chapter 63

At the bottom of the Easton's driveway, Nicky Geraci got back behind the wheel of the black Lincoln MKS, with Easton taking the front passenger seat.

Dixon Shaw had waited in the back seat while Geraci retrieved Easton from the house.

"Good evening, Dix," said Easton.

"Chet. Sorry to get you out so late."

Geraci slipped the car into drive, and moved down the street populated with large residential homes that had been built within the past decade.

Chet said, "Not a worry, after all, this is Vegas, right?"

"It is. But I know that late-night Vegas isn't exactly your thing."

"I don't mind, really. Gets me away from Angelica."

"Things still rough between you two?"

"Yes, unfortunately, and I'm weighing the costs and benefits, and coming to the realization that it's not going to improve. It's going to be a net loss over the long run."

"Well, you never know how people can change. Sometimes they surprise you."

"Maybe," said Chet. "But I've found that people usually are unwilling to change in any significant ways, even when it's obvious that things could improve if they did. They just can't make the calculation."

"Well, I'm still sorry for getting you out late."

"Like I said, Dix, it is not an issue, especially when you're talking about improvements at The River. What are you thinking?"

"I've got something significant in mind."

"Really? Well, as long as the numbers add up."

"There's always a cost involved, so I'm not sure you're going to like all of this."

"When I'm pulled out of the house late at night with Dixon Shaw, I know it's a big idea that's going to be nicely profitable."

They drove for a few minutes in silence.

Nicky asked, "How's Jennifer doing, Dix?"

Chet added, "Yes, how is she?"

"She's getting stronger, I think. But she's still not in the clear."

Chapter 64

Paige started the silver Equinox, and backed out of the parking space in the hospital garage.

She screeched up to the parking attendant gate, handed him a parking slip and a ten-dollar bill. "Open the gate, fast."

The heavyset man in the booth protested, "But don't you want your change? You only owe a buck fifty."

"Keep the change, and open the fucking gate," commanded Caldwell.

The attendant obliged, and Paige hit the gas.

Stephen asked her, "Do you know where The River site is?"

"Yes. Found it while checking up on Shaw. We'll be there in 15 minutes."

"And are we armed?"

"I can't believe you just asked that question. Since the FBI took back the guns we used at the ranch, Charlie got us rearmed through an old CIA buddy. I might have forgotten to mention that we shot up the front door to Shaw's penthouse in order to get in."

"Yes, that slipped your mind."

"Case on the backseat has the three Glocks, magazines and knives."

Grant grabbed and pulled the silver attaché up front, resting it on his lap. He opened it. "Almost like old times, Paige."

She smirked. "Right, except that you're married, we're trying to save your father-in-law, and we're no longer with the CIA or sleeping together. Other than that, just like old times."

"Yeah, well, there's that."

They drove in silence for a few minutes, until Grant's phone buzzed. It was Ron.

"Ron, what is it? Are you at the hospital?"

"Stephen, you have to get back here now."

The fear and concern in McDermott's voice was unmistakable.

"What is it? What's happening?"

"Her blood pressure was suddenly falling, and her heart rate became erratic. I just got here, but can't get in the room. They've got a team in there, working on her. I can see a little through the curtains. You better come back immediately."

God, please not this. I'm begging your healing. Please.

He looked at Paige, who was eyeing him as she drove on to The River.

What do I do?

Ron said, "Stephen?"

I have to go back, obviously, right?

Ron asked, "Stephen, are you there? Did you hear what I just said? Get back here."

But ... but? What do you mean "but"? She's your wife, your love. Get the hell back there. But what about her father? I can't let the man die.

Stephen said, "Ron, I..." He stopped.

"Stephen, what are you doing?" declared Father Ron McDermott.

I can only help Jen with prayer. She's in the doctor's hands, in God's hands. But I can save her father, and that's what she'd expect me to do.

"Ron, I can't come back there right now."

"Stephen, what did you just say? Have you lost it?"

"Please stay with her, and I'll call you back as soon as I can."

"Are you crazy? What could you possibly be doing that would keep you away from Jennifer now?"

Trust me, my friend.

Stephen took a deep breath. "I'm going to save her father's life."

Grant ended the call, and put his phone away. He slipped a magazine into each of the guns. He stared straight ahead in silence.

Sweet Jesus, please be with my Jennifer.

Paige took out her phone, and said, "I'm calling Noack to get his FBI ass to the site."

Grant replied coolly, "Fine. Step on it."

Chapter 65

Geraci turned the car into the construction site marked by a big sign declaring "Coming Soon ... The River Park and Resort!"

He drove some 30 yards, with high fences on each side, to a gate, which his assistant slid open.

Geraci stopped and opened the window. "Stay here. We're going to go over a few things. Not sure how long it'll take."

The assistant replied, "Of course, Mr. Geraci."

The window went up, and the car moved ahead, making a few turns around various vehicles, equipment and supplies.

Geraci parked the car not far from an idling concrete mixer truck with its turning drum, and the place where the foundation was about to be laid for a rock mountain that would host two rivers – one for a gentle boat ride and the other for a more adventurous kayak-like experience – emanating from a giant waterfall that would emerge from the main, massive hotel building. The hotel portion of the structure was nearly complete.

The three men got out of the car in silence. Geraci moved around front and leaned against the grill of the Lincoln, with Shaw to his right and Easton to his left.

Easton looked at Shaw and said, "Well, Dix, what's the deal?"

Dix tightened his fists. "Why, Chet? What did you do it for?"

Easton calmly replied, "Did what, Dix?"

Shaw screamed, "Stop the bullshit! Why did you have Jennifer kidnapped, and why the hell did you want me dead?"

Easton said, "You arrogant asshole." The anger in his voice made his nasally tone worse. "You always have to be calling the shots, don't you? Well, enough already. You need to get out of the way so this company can become what it should be."

"What are you talking about?"

"You're in the way of this becoming a leading global gaming company."

"Is this about my decision not to go public?" Dix asked incredulously.

"Yes! Your decision. What gives you the right to limit the future of our company?"

Shaw chuckled. "Sixty percent ownership, that's what gives me the right. I thought you understood numbers, Chet?"

Easton said, "I do understand the numbers. It's you, Dix, who doesn't get the numbers. We go public, expand in the right emerging markets, and this little, rinky-dink firm becomes a global leader, and we join the incredibly wealthy. Not just doing well, but Forbes-list rich. But you just say no, and that's supposed to be it? I don't think so."

"Well, I do think so, Chet. And after you're dead, we'll make sure that Angelica goes away happy, and Nicky and I will split your 20 percent." Shaw pulled out a handgun from its resting place in the belt against his back, and pointed it at Easton. "But before I kill you, Chet, and fittingly make you a permanent addition to The River" – he motioned with the gun to the concrete truck and then at the place where the resort would be completed – "tell me why you grabbed Jennifer, and had her beaten. I assume you eventually were going to have my daughter killed as well."

Easton's small laugh sounded more like the snort of a pig. "Actually, Dix, Jennifer was not part of the plan."

"What do you mean?" asked Shaw.

Geraci interjected, "Sorry about that, Dix. That was Gil Rice going too far. He wanted to hurt you by offing your daughter because he thought that you killed his son."

There was a split-second delay before Dix turned to see Geraci pointing a gun at his head.

Shaw's shoulders sagged ever so slightly. "Two Gloves, no."

Geraci smiled. "Sorry again, Dix, but yes."

"After everything we've been through?"

"Yeah, Dix, and that's the problem. We're supposed to make it big, real big. Chet sees the opportunities, the numbers. I see them. But you don't. Rice and his team were supposed to do the dirty work on you. When that failed, we were going to take some time, you know, to regroup. But things kept pushing us. Your son-in-law didn't help, and framing that guy, Clark, that Grant screwed over didn't work. It's still a little dicey, but seems that it'll work out anyway. We get your 60 percent, as per our agreement since you're not married, and you disappear. It'll get hot for a bit, but without a body, just like with Ollie Rice, the case eventually will go cold and be filed away."

"You disloyal son of a bitch."

"Now, now, before you get too excited, drop that gun."

Easton pulled out his own pistol as well. "Yes, we have the numbers now, so toss the gun aside."

Dix dropped the weapon.

Chapter 66

Caldwell slowed down as she approached the entrance to The River site, and turned the SUV past the "Coming Soon" sign.

The vehicle's headlights revealed a man standing on the other side of a gate. She let the Equinox inch forward.

Stephen said, "That's Geraci's right hand man. Standing guard, no doubt."

Paige observed, "Well, so much for stealth. We'll have to go with surprise."

"Agreed."

Paige grabbed one of the guns with her right hand, and transferred it to her left. Grant picked up a Glock as well. Caldwell hit the gas hard, and swerved adroitly around a huge pothole. They each hit buttons to lower their windows.

As the SUV accelerated, Geraci's assistant pulled a gun from inside his jacket. He had time to get off two shots – one missed wildly and the other took out a headlight.

As the Equinox got closer, Geraci's assistant moved to the side of the gate, and raised his gun once more.

He was on Paige's side of the vehicle. She declared, "He's mine."

The Equinox hit the gate. As chain link fence flew into the air, Caldwell fired off three shots. The first flew high, but the second and third found their marks – the shoulder and stomach of Geraci's assistant. He tumbled to the ground, and would bleed out in minutes.

Paige said, "Crashing through a fence and taking down a target at the same time. Not bad, wouldn't you say?"

"Are you fishing for compliments?"

Caldwell slowed the SUV slightly in order to start moving around the various construction site obstacles, and shut off the remaining lights on the vehicle. "No, but a little recognition of excellence would be nice."

As they came around the base of a crane, Stephen saw the three men standing in a triangle, with two pointing guns. "Crap."

Grant swung open his door as Caldwell drove at the standoff. In one smooth motion, he moved onto his feet, leaned out the door, and grabbed the ceiling bar above the passenger door with his left hand. Hanging out the door, Grant raised the Glock in his right hand, and fired at Geraci.

The engine noise and gunshot meant that Geraci, Easton and Shaw all turned their heads at Grant and Caldwell.

After Grant's shot whizzed by, Geraci returned two shots, with one hitting the SUV's windshield.

Paige stopped the vehicle, opened her door and used it for cover. She fired off two shots at Geraci, who started moving away from the scene.

However, Chet Easton's gun never moved from Dixon Shaw. Dix looked at Chet for a fraction of a second, and then moved to pick up the gun tossed on the ground in front of him.

Easton didn't flinch, and pulled the trigger.

The bullet ripped into Shaw's hip, and he fell to the ground. Easton started walking closer to Shaw.

Geraci fired additional shots in the direction of the SUV, as he moved for cover behind the concrete truck. Another shot from Paige ricocheted off the truck.

Grant's attention went to Easton, who was approaching the fallen Dixon Shaw.

Easton was 40 yards away from Grant, and it was dark. Stephen had made more difficult shots than this before. But that was a long time ago.

I've got this.

As he released his breath, Grant pulled the trigger.

The bullet entered the side of Chet Easton's head just below the right eye. Easton toppled to the ground. His shattered, blood-splattered glasses flew off and came to rest next to the gun that Dixon Shaw had tried to pick up.

Grant's attention shifted back to Geraci.

Where is he? He stepped down onto the dirt, staying behind the passenger door of the Equinox.

He looked over at Paige. "Behind the truck," she said. She leaned into the vehicle, and grabbed two more cartridges and slipped them into a side pocket of her cargo pants. Paige then signaled to Stephen her intention to move across the open area between the SUV and the concrete truck. "Cover me."

Grant started to protest, but knew it would be fruitless. So, as Caldwell moved out from behind the SUV, Grant fired shots at the rear of the truck.

Paige stopped next to the large, front tire.

No good staying here. After quickly reaching back inside the SUV, Grant sprinted at the truck as well, and finished behind the double rear tires.

Paige signaled to move on three, counting down with her fingers.

Grant slipped around the back of the truck, and Paige the front. But at her second step, the engine and gears of the truck roared, and the vehicle lunged forward.

Paige skidded on the dirt, and fell onto her back. As the truck moved above her, she rolled away from the tires, and laid out flat on the ground as the massive truck lurched ahead.

Grant started running after the truck, but hesitated as he saw Paige's body emerge on the ground. But when she rolled on her stomach, and pointed her gun at the truck and fired, Grant accelerated his sprint.

Behind the wheel of the mixer, Geraci steered around the crane, shifted into a higher gear, and picked up speed. Grant was now running full stride. Just before Geraci smashed the truck through a stack of two-by-fours, Grant was able to grab the rail on a side ladder leading up to the passenger side door, and pulled himself clear of the flying debris. In the process, he had to drop the Glock. The gun bounced away from the truck.

Grant moved up the ladder, reached higher and pulled open the passenger side door. He leaned back and clear as Geraci fired off two shots in his direction.

The truck moved by the lifeless body of Geraci's assistant, and barreled down the fenced lane, heading to the exit of The River site.

Grant yelled, "Nicky, you can stop this truck, or you can die, which is it?"

"You going to kill me, Pastor? Dying's not an option, at least not for me. Looks like you're the one in trouble."

The truck picked up more speed.

Got to make a move before he gets this thing out on the road.

From his back pocket, Grant pulled out the tactical knife he had grabbed from the SUV. Then he spotted the pothole quickly approaching that Paige had missed on the way in.

Grant flipped open the blade of the knife. Just as the truck was about to strike the pothole, Grant climbed the remaining steps of the ladder. When the truck hit the deep crevice in the road and bounced sharply, Geraci's attention was momentarily drawn back to the road and steering wheel.

Those fractional seconds were all that Grant needed. He leaped in the door and across the cab, leading with the knife.

Geraci deflected Grant's first thrust, and tried to direct his gun at Grant.

But Grant was able to push Geraci's arm, and the shot missed.

As the two men struggled, Geraci pushed down on the gas pedal, and the truck accelerated. When it careened onto the road, two approaching SUVs screeched to a halt.

As he watched the truck streak in front of him, FBI Special Agent Rich Noack said, "Shit, that's not good."

The truck plowed through a low wooden fence into the parking lot of a small shopping center, heading straight for the darkened stores.

Inside the runaway concrete mixer, Grant, with his left hand, managed to pull Geraci's right arm across his body. But Geraci pulled back. The gun fell to the floor of the cab, and all Grant could hang on to was one of Geraci's gloves.

Nicky Two Gloves Geraci's gloveless, shriveled, deformed, multicolored hand reached back, and grabbed a hunk of Grant's hair.

Stephen ignored the pain in his scalp, and with his free right hand, he positioned the knife's point against Geraci's chest.

Geraci yelled, and managed to get both hands on Grant's head, pulling and scratching.

But Grant whispered coolly in his opponent's ear, "No one hurts my family."

Grant shoved the knife through flesh and into Geraci's heart. He turned the weapon, and pulled it sideways.

Geraci's hands fell away from Grant's head, and his body went limp.

Grant refocused on the approaching building. His foot found the brake, and he whipped the wheel to the right.

The physics did not work. The truck tumbled onto its side, and slid through a frozen yogurt shop and the pizza parlor next door. The truck came out the other side of the building, and eventually slowed to a stop, with concrete flowing out of the drum.

Caldwell had been pursuing the truck on foot. As she ran past the apparently amazed Noack, as well as Trent Nguyen and Jessica West, she called out and pointed back from where she had come, "Shaw's been shot. Get someone over there."

Noack ordered two agents in the direction Paige indicated, and then he, Nguyen and West went after Caldwell.

Paige paused at the front of the destroyed stores, and shifted direction, heading around the building to get to the truck.

By the time she reached the mixer, Grant had already climbed out of the broken front windshield.

"Stephen, are you okay?"

The right half of his shirt, including the sleeve, was torn away. Cuts marked his face, arms, chest and back, but nothing was broken.

"I survived. Geraci didn't." Grant still had the knife in his hand. He flipped the blade closed, and handed it to Paige.

Noack, Nguyen and West arrived. Noack said, "What the hell happened?"

Grant replied, "Paige can fill you in, and I'll talk later." He turned to Paige. "Dix?"

She nodded. "He's hit, but he's going to make it. I'll get him to the hospital."

Grant said, "Thanks." He turned to Noack. "Right now, I need to get to my wife."

Noack said, "Come on, Pastor Grant, we'll get you there."

Chapter 67

Stephen Grant entered his wife's ICU room. The sight hit him harder than any physical blow ever could.

One of Jennifer's eyes was open, with the other still swollen shut, but her face offered a tired, weak smile.

A wave of happiness and relief smothered Grant. Emotions flooded every part of his body, mind and soul. Tears flowed from his eyes, and he had lost the ability to speak.

Jennifer turned her left hand over and opened it. She softly said, "My love."

Stephen stumbled forward. He cradled and gently kissed Jennifer's open hand, tears falling on her wrist.

Both Ron and Joan, who had been at Jen's side, moved out of the room.

Stephen looked up at Jennifer's bruised and beaten face, and smiled broadly.

Noack had provided Grant with an FBI t-shirt to replace the remnants of his own shirt. But Jennifer squinted at the scratches on his face. "Stephen, what happened to you?"

He took a deep breath. "So much, Jen, and I'm going to tell you everything. But maybe it should wait a bit. You need to get stronger."

She shook her head slightly. "No, I need to know. And where's my father? Has he been here?"

Stephen relayed the essentials of what had occurred over the previous two-plus days since she had been kidnapped.

When Stephen said that Gil Rice had been killed when they raided the ranch, Jennifer squeezed his hand. She whispered, "How did he die?"

Deciding that the full details could wait, Stephen cleared his throat, and answered, "Paige. Paige shot him."

Jennifer eased her grip, and rubbed Stephen's hand gently. "I see."

"Jen, there's more."

"Tell me, please."

When Stephen explained that both Nicky Geraci and Chet Easton were involved, Jennifer went back to squeezing his hand. She said, "God, no. Why?"

Stephen said that her father was the real target.

Jennifer said, "Dad? Is he all right?"

"Jen, Dix has been shot. But he's going to be okay." Stephen went on to give the broad details of what had just happened at The River construction site.

Jennifer was silent for more than a minute, with the one eye she could manage to open kept closed.

Stephen finally said, "Jen, I'm so sorry about all of this."

She said, "Sorry? Stephen, my love and my guardian, you saved my father. You saved me. What could you possibly be sorry about?"

I hope you still say that when I tell you everything that happened.

Stephen said, "I don't know about that. But I do know that I'm here for you now, and will do everything I can to help you."

Jen smiled again. "Well, my pastor husband, I understand you might have an 'in' on the prayer front. That would certainly help."

Stephen returned the smile, but there was element of sadness hidden behind it.

Lord, do I still have an "in"? Can you possibly forgive what I've done? Can you forgive me for what I can't imagine forgiving myself – being willing to murder and driving Paige to act so I didn't? My head says you will; my heart has doubts. Can Jennifer forgive this? And then there's my mind saying that I should be seeking forgiveness for other acts, but my conscience saying the opposite, that I don't need to be sorry. Not sorry in the least.

"Stephen?"

Jennifer's voice snapped him out of his conflicted feelings of guilt, or the lack thereof. "Jen, yes, sorry."

"A prayer?"

"Of course," he said. He cradled Jennifer's hand once more, and lowered his head. "Almighty God, our Father, thank you for your generosity and healing. Thank you for bringing Jennifer into my life in the first place, and for her being here right now." His voice broke, but he continued. "Thank you for all of the people, the friends new and old, who helped Jennifer and helped me in recent days. Please continue the healing process for Jennifer and for Dix. By the work of the Holy Spirit, help us to understand, appreciate and give thanks for everything you have accomplished, and given to us. We are not deserving, we have all sinned – I have sinned – but your grace abounds, inexplicably. Grant us forgiveness, though we are undeserving." Grant was pleading for himself. "We pray this through your Son, Jesus Christ our Lord, who lives and reigns with you and the Holy Spirit, one God, now and forever."

Stephen allowed his head to drop into Jennifer's open hand.

She whispered, "Amen," and moved her hand on top of his head. She gently rubbed his hair.

Father, thank you for bringing her back to me. I need her, desperately. More now than ever before if I'm going to find my way to live with all I've done.

Grant stood up and moved a chair closer to Jen's bed. He sat down, took his wife's hand, and looked at the clock on the wall. It was 15 minutes after midnight. *Sunday morning.* Exhaustion suddenly swept over him. *When was the last time I slept?*

"Jen, are you okay?"

"I am now." She struggled a bit to turn her head to look at Stephen. "Why don't you go to sleep for a while?"

"Not a bad idea."

Stephen quickly drifted off.

Chapter 68

It was 7:30 on Sunday morning, and Paige Caldwell, Charlie Driessen and Rich Noack were reviewing what had happened in recent days over coffee in a pastry shop on the ground floor of Casino Beach.

Charlie said, "It's just so damn messy. I don't like messy."

"Completely agree. Too many loose ends," observed Noack. "Where the hell is Eric Clark?"

Charlie interrupted, "You mean, where is Eric Clark's body?"

"Unfortunately, you're probably right. And the same goes for Oliver Rice. I don't like murder cases without bodies."

Paige added, "Geraci and Easton are no longer among the breathing to give us those answers."

Noack said, "But I want the answers."

Paige smiled. "Yes, well, Rich, we don't always get what we want."

"Yeah, thanks for that."

Driessen said, "I'm going to ask what no one else seems to want to ask: What's Dixon Shaw's role in all of this? Okay, he was the target for Easton and Geraci over just how rich they all wanted to get. But he was the boss when Oliver Rice disappeared. He's also the father of a woman who was kidnapped, and I assume like us, Shaw was pointed in the direction of Clark."

Noack said, "Believe me, we've thought about all of that. The local FBI office is going to dig more on Dixon Shaw, and the cases of Oliver Rice and Eric Clark. I can't speak for the local cops."

Driessen turned to Paige. "What's Grant going to say about his father-in-law?"

She finished her coffee, and answered curtly, "No real clue." Paige asked Noack, "What about Jonas Locke and his wife? Anything more on that front?"

Noack said, "Not sure. I have to check with the San Francisco office. You said that Locke did work with McEnany?"

"Yes," answered Paige.

"Everything I know about McEnany tells me that the FBI would benefit from asking what's the latest he has on the bombing."

Neither Caldwell nor Driessen responded.

Noack drained the bottom of his coffee cup. "I've got to get going. There's more to do in the local office, and Nguyen and I should be heading back to D.C. tomorrow morning. What are you two up to?"

Paige said, "I'm not much for this city. I'm going to try to grab a flight back to D.C. tonight."

Driessen said, "Not me. I'm not only going to get a couple more hotel nights out of Dixon Shaw, but I'm going to take a little of his money at the blackjack tables."

Noack stood up from the table, and slipped on the dark blue suit jacket that had been draped over the back of his chair.

Noack shook Charlie's hand. "Good luck at the tables, Driessen."

"Thanks."

Noack turned to Caldwell, and they gave each other a brief hug. He said, "I'd say stay out of trouble, Paige, but I know that's not going to happen. But at least stay on the right side of the law."

She smiled, "Don't I always, Rich?"

He laughed. "I know better."

Chapter 69

Paige finished pinning up her long black hair, and moved over to the mirror to look at the new sleeveless, polka dot dress she had just bought in one of the resort's shops.

She nodded in approval.

As she zipped her duffle bag closed, there was a knock at her hotel room door. She opened it to see Stephen Grant.

"My goodness, Pastor Grant, why ever are you knocking on my hotel room door?" She batted her eyelids.

Based on their past, Stephen knew that Paige enjoyed teasing. Still, it tended to bother him.

"Hi, Paige. Can I come in?"

"That depends. Are your intentions honorable?"

With a trace of exasperation in his voice, he said, "Paige, please."

"Honorable as ever. You can come in anyway."

Grant moved into the room. "I wanted to catch you before you left."

Paige asked, "How is Jennifer?"

"Much better. I left her with Joan and Ron early this morning, and went back to the hotel for a little shut eye, a shower, and something to eat. They called a little while ago. Jennifer's being moved out of ICU."

"That's good news."

"It is. I was on my way there, but wanted to stop by for a minute."

He turned, walked over to the window, and stood in silence.

Paige said, "Charlie and I met with Noack this morning."

"Anything new?"

"Not really," she replied. "Everybody's frustrated at not being able to pin down the details on what actually happened to Oliver Rice and Eric Clark."

Stephen did not reply.

Paige continued, "I didn't share your gut feeling that Dix had Clark killed. But the same thing has occurred to the FBI, and they're going to continue investigating."

"Good."

"Good?"

"Yes, that provides me a little relief from the idea that I might be keeping something of value from them."

Paige sat on the edge of the bed and crossed her legs. "Have you told Jennifer about your gut feeling?"

"No, I haven't." He continued to look out the window at a Las Vegas drenched in bright sunlight.

"Are you going to tell her?"

"I don't know."

Paige broke another several seconds of silence. "Stephen, why are you here?"

Grant grabbed a chair from the corner of the room, and dragged it over so he could sit face to face with Paige. He looked into her blue eyes.

Her discomfort was evident to Stephen by a brief look away, and the unfolding of her legs to place each foot on the carpet.

"I know you're going to mock me again, but I'm torn up about Gil Rice."

"Stephen..."

"No, let me talk. You came when I needed you, without question or hesitation. You risked your life for me, and for Jennifer. And when I was about to cross the line, you crossed it instead. I don't know what to do with that."

"We've been over this. How about accepting the fact that I'm okay with it? In fact, I'd do it again to the little shit if I had the chance."

"Yes, I know you would. But that doesn't change the fact that if it weren't for my own uncontrollable anger, my desire to punish, you would not have been put in that situation in the first place."

Paige sighed. "Life was simpler when we were partners. Stephen, this is not an issue for me. Gil Rice kidnapped and beat your wife nearly to death. He deserved the bullet he got. I know a part of you agrees with that. But that pastor side of you is wrestling with it."

They stared at each other.

She continued, "I understand this much: You could not pull that trigger given where you sit in life. But I could."

"It doesn't work that way. An act, especially this one, cannot be wrong for me but okay for you."

"Well, we'll have to agree to disagree on that, my dear, because that's exactly how I see it."

"That's not helping."

"Stephen, I can help you in a lot of ways, but sorting out some kind of moral angst over shooting that bastard lies beyond my skill set. I can't help you with that."

Grant managed a smile. "Well, can you at least forgive me?"

Paige grunted. "If you need to hear me say that, then, yes, I forgive you."

Stephen said, "Thanks." At the same time, he knew that she could not fathom why he desired forgiveness for what he had done to her.

He stood up, and moved the chair back to the corner. "When is your flight?"

"In a couple of hours. By the way, how did you know I was leaving today?"

Grant smiled, "Because I remember how much you dislike Las Vegas from the last time we were here."

"Long time ago. That was quite a mission."

"It was."

"I'm surprised they let you come back."

"Things pass with time, I guess."

Paige walked over, and kissed his cheek. "Time tends to do that healing thing. Now, go be with Jennifer."

"Thanks again, for everything."

As he opened the door, Paige said, "Tell Jennifer that she owes me, big time."

Stephen said, "She knows."

He shut the door.

Paige whispered, "No, I don't think she fully knows."

Chapter 70

It was late Sunday afternoon in San Francisco when Sean McEnany's flight touched down.

He had been traveling for nearly twelve hours, flying from Las Américas International Airport in the Dominican Republic to Mineta San Jose International Airport. The journey was made easier flying on the personal Gulfstream jet of a Silicon Valley colleague. He was able to get some sleep, while also tracking the target via his computer.

His software colleague also provided McEnany with ground transportation in the form of a blue Dodge Charger. The drive north on US-101 to San Francisco took less than 45 minutes.

McEnany parked the car in a lot near AT&T Park, home of the Giants, and walked along San Francisco Bay toward Fisherman's Wharf. He glanced at the readout on his smartphone that tracked the location of the target's phone.

McEnany's man was still in his hotel, a nondescript, chain lodge just two blocks from the water. The man registered under the name Quinn Buchholz.

As he approached the hotel, McEnany pulled a San Francisco Giants hat from one pocket of the black jacket he was wearing, and large, dark sunglasses from the other. After putting both on, he zipped up the front of the jacket, and turned up the collar. He already had the room number for Mr. Buchholz, so he didn't break stride passing the front desk. McEnany also had reviewed where all of the security cameras were, and positioned his head and body accordingly.

He kept his head down on the elevator ride to the third floor as well.

The doors opened. McEnany again moved strategically down the hall, turned a corner, and came to Room 311.

Turning away from the lone camera in this part of the hallway, he pulled his Glock G30S with a suppressor attached from underneath his jacket and shirt.

McEnany put his ear close to the door. The sound of a shower running was clear. He smiled, and pulled a small device from his pocket. A flat card extended from a black rectangular box with three small lights. McEnany inserted the card into the hotel door keycard slot, and pushed a button on the side of the device. Two red lights flickered, and then went off, giving way to a constant green light. He pulled the device out of the lock, and the door clicked.

McEnany opened the door in silence, and slipped inside, with the gun leading the way.

As the shower ran, McEnany scanned the rest of the small room. No one else was there.

He pushed open the bathroom door. His target was humming behind the shower curtain.

While leveling the gun at the shower curtain, McEnany announced, "Mr. Buchholz? Room service."

The man said, "What the hell?" He poked his head out from behind the curtain, with his long brown hair dripping wet. Seeing McEnany and the gun, his next utterance was, "Oh, shit."

McEnany said, "This is for Jonas and Peggy Locke, as well as their two children."

McEnany fired one shot that ripped through the shower curtain, and entered his target's chest. The man crashed to the floor of the shower.

McEnany approached the shower, and pulled the curtain aside. The man's eyes focused on McEnany's gun. Two more shots in the chest drained the life from the eyes of the man who murdered McEnany's friend.

McEnany did not bother to shut off the water. The spray of water fell on the dead man's chest, washing away the blood as it emerged from the three chest holes.

McEnany carefully retraced his steps, until reaching the ground floor, where he left via a side exit of the hotel.

The Giants hat and dark jacket were removed, and he suddenly appeared as a very different person with short blond hair and a bright blue polo shirt.

The jacket, hat and sunglasses were strategically deposited in separate receptacles blocks away from the hotel. He kept the gun.

McEnany stopped in the team store at the ballpark, selecting gifts for the family.

After getting back in the Charger, he pulled out his smartphone and called his wife. "Hi, Rach. Are you guys all checked in?"

He listened.

"Yes, I'm done with work. I'm leaving the city now, and I'll be at the inn in about an hour and 15. Maybe we can grab dinner in Carmel."

Sean listened again.

"Sounds good. Love you."

McEnany hung up. He started the Charger, pulled out of the parking lot, crossed over the Lefty O'Doul Bridge, and went past AT&T Park and the statues of Juan Marichal, his leg kick high in the air, and Willie Mays, heading to the entrance for I-280 South.

Chapter 71

When Stephen arrived at the hospital, Jennifer had already been moved to a new room.

The attendant at the front desk looked at her computer screen, smiled, and said, "Let me see, Mr. Grant." Stephen was dressed in a blue oxford button down shirt and tan pants, with no signs that he was a pastor. She continued, "Yes, Mrs. Grant is now in Suite 3 in the Shaw Pavilion."

"I'm sorry, did you say the Shaw Pavilion?"

"Oh, yes. The Dixon Shaw Pavilion. It's very nice."

Grant chuckled to himself. *I'm sure it is. How did I miss The Dixon Shaw Pavilion earlier?*

The attendant gave him quick directions to a separate elevator that went directly to the top floor of the hospital.

When the doors opened, he stepped into what looked like a completely different building. It had the unmistakable feel of a very upscale hotel.

A young woman with long blond hair, wearing a red blazer, was sitting inside a large, circular, maple wood desk. Metallic letters were mounted around the desk, spelling out, "The Dixon Shaw Pavilion."

"Hello, may I help you?" she queried.

"Yes, hello. I'm looking for my wife, Jennifer Grant."

She smiled brightly. "Of course, Pastor Grant. Your wife, Dr. Grant, is in Suite 3." She rose from her chair and came out of the circular desk. "Please follow me." She led

Stephen down one of two long hallways. Their movements made little noise, as all sound seemed to be absorbed by the deep carpeting, and textured walls.

The woman stopped just short of Suite 3. She said, "Here you are, Pastor Grant."

"Thank you," he glanced at her nametag, "Melanie."

"You're quite welcome. Please don't hesitate to ask me for any assistance." She turned, and headed back to her desk.

Suite 3 turned out to be much larger than Stephen had expected. It was brightly lit, with afternoon sun streaming in through large windows. It also was well equipped, including a small kitchen, two deep armchairs, a couch, various tables with fresh flowers, three floor-to-ceiling bookcases, two armoires, and two wall-mounted televisions. The room was not a single. There were two beds. Jennifer was asleep in one. Dixon Shaw was immobilized in the second, given the operation on his side, which wound up including a replaced hip.

"Pastor," Dix announced in a whisper. "Hope you didn't mind me instructing them to bring Jennifer up here after being released from ICU?"

Grant walked over to his father-in-law, and stopped at the foot of the bed. "Ah, I guess not. It certainly looks like this is the best care available."

"You can count on that. The best in Vegas. I've made sure of that."

"Right, The Dixon Shaw Pavilion?"

"Well, it's important to give back, right?"

"Yes, it is." Stephen moved to the side of the bed, closer to Dix. He lowered his voice to a whisper. "In fact, given everything that's happened, seems like we all might need to do a little confessing and seeking forgiveness."

Shaw matched Grant's whisper. "Think so, do you? Why do you have to seek forgiveness, Pastor?"

"Well, let's just say that I made a bad decision, or two. Not thinking clearly, and putting someone else in a no-win situation."

"Hmmm, I might be able to understand that. But were your decisions made with the best intentions, specifically, were you protecting Jennifer?"

"Yes, I was."

"Then don't worry about it."

"It's not that easy."

"It should be."

"But what about you, Dix?"

"What about me?"

"Anything over the last three days that you shouldn't have done, that you might need forgiveness for?"

"Forgiveness? No. I made a bad call. But given the information I had, it was the right decision at the time."

"Did that bad call have to do with either Oliver Rice or Eric Clark?"

Shaw's eyes narrowed as he looked at Grant. Seconds went by.

Is he going to come clean with me? I can't imagine it, but you never know.

Dix finally said, "Most certainly not. Seems clear that the cases of Oliver Rice, his father, Gil, and your Eric Clark all trace back to my so-called partners and friends, Geraci and Easton."

Stephen started to respond, but was cut short by Shaw, who elevated his voice notably. "By the way, forgive me for not saying so immediately, but thank you. You and Ms. Caldwell saved my life. I'll never be able to repay what I owe you."

"You're welcome, Dix, but you certainly don't owe me anything." *Let's not get off track. I want to dig a bit more.*

"I think I do."

"I think you do, too, Dad." Jennifer's voice had grown stronger, though it was still far lower than usual and sounded sleepy.

Stephen quickly turned and moved next to her. "Jen, how are you feeling?"

"Well, everything pretty much still hurts. But I can start moving parts of my body that wouldn't budge last night. My head's cleared up more, and I can almost open this other eye. I guess this is progress?"

"It is. Relax. It's going to take time. But we're going to get you fixed up, and back home."

She managed a smile. "I so want to go back to our home."

Stephen replied, "Me, too. Although, this isn't a bad room that you and your father have here."

"It's very nice. I told him it was unnecessary, but he insisted."

From the other side of the room, Dix said, "Of course it was necessary, Jenny. My own business partners were behind everything that happened to you."

"I know, Dad. I still can't believe it."

Dix replied, "Me, either."

The three were silent for a few minutes. Then Dix said, "Jenny, I have to tell you something, and then ask a question."

"Okay."

"This is a big life thing. Are you up for it, or do you want to wait until we both can at least get out of bed under our own strength?"

What's this about?

Jennifer answered, "Put it that way, and you know that I can't wait. What is it?"

"I've already had the ownership papers on the casino company changed to reflect that both Nicky and Chet are dead. And as long as Easton's wife, Angelica, had nothing to do with their plot, I'll buy out her 20 percent, making her quite comfortable in life."

"Okay, but what does that have to do with me?"

"I'm giving you 40 percent of the firm."

Stephen and Jennifer replied with the same word at the same time: "What?"

Jen continued, "No, Dad, that's not..."

Dix interrupted, "It should have been done long ago. And that's the very least of what I owe you. I am so sorry that I left you out... no, that I pushed you out of my life. I've come to realize, finally, how I did that, Jenny. I not only hurt your mom by what I did, I hurt our family, and that means I hurt you. You were right all along. When I cheated on your mother, I cheated on you as well. I'm so sorry for that."

Stephen watched as Dixon Shaw's eyes moistened, and a small tear formed in the corner of Jen's less-swollen eye.

Jennifer said, "Dad, I don't know what to say."

Stephen looked at his wife. *She really doesn't know what to say, and neither do I.*

"I know, Jenny. But there's one more thing. I not only don't want to push you away any longer, I want you, and of course, you, Pastor, in my life. Jenny, I could see the surprise on your face at dinner the other night when I mentioned that I always wanted you to be part of running the casino business. I meant it, and I should have said it to you directly and clearly long ago. And now that you're going to be 40-percent owner, you should be involved in running this entire operation."

Is he kidding?

"Dad, I ..."

Dix help up a hand. "Wait, please. I know this is coming out of nowhere for you. But I'm very serious."

Okay, he's not kidding.

Stephen's father-in-law continued, "Among the things I've learned in recent hours is that the only people you can truly trust are family."

Whoa, Dix talking trust and family. I know Jen is factoring in the irony there.

Dix concluded, "I need you, Jenny. Like I said the other night, you'd be the ideal person to run The River."

Jennifer started, "Dad, I really..."

Shaw said, "Don't answer me now. You've been through too much. If you could just think about it for a while, and the two of you discuss it, that's all I can ask."

Jennifer took Stephen's hand, and said to her father, "Dad, Stephen and I will certainly think about and discuss it."

"That's great. Thank you."

On cue, there was a knock at the door, and in came Father Ron McDermott and Joan Kraus.

Stephen didn't realize how much he needed the diversions of friendship, stories, jokes, and laughs that followed over the following couple of hours.

Chapter 72

It was a little after 10:30 PM when Stephen left the hospital suite, after both Jennifer and Dix had fallen asleep.

He had promised to meet Ron at The Twenties for a nightcap or two. But before heading over to a cab idling at the curb, Grant pulled out his phone and called Sean McEnany.

"Hello, Pastor. How's Jennifer?"

"Sean, she's improved a lot."

"That's so good to hear."

"Thanks, and thank you so much for what you did for her. You, Paige and Charlie helped save her life."

"You're welcome, Pastor. But like Paige and Charlie, I couldn't do any less for both of you."

"Well, I can't adequately express my gratitude." Stephen then asked, "Can I impose on you for one more favor?"

"Of course. What is it?"

"I know that during the heat of all that's been going on, you were poking around into Dixon Shaw's background."

"Yes, Paige and I thought it wise."

"You were right. Would you mind picking up where you left off, and going as deep as possible into his history, relationships, and so on?"

"Are you sure that Jennifer and you want to know everything that might come up?"

"Sean, just a few days ago, I never would have asked you to do this, and I know Jennifer would not have wanted the full story on her father. But things have changed."

"They certainly have."

"In more ways than you know. I'll explain more fully at some point. But I need to know everything, and whether she wants to or not, Jennifer will need to know everything as well."

"No problem. But I've taken a few days with the family in Carmel in California. Can this wait, or do you need me on this immediately?"

"Of course not. Enjoy the time with Rachel and the kids." Then another thought dawned on Stephen. "California? My God, Sean, forgive my thoughtlessness. I am so sorry about your friend and his wife. That was horrible."

"It was. Thanks, Pastor."

"How are their children?"

"I'm not sure. But I know they're with Jonas's sister-in-law."

"Anything on the bomber?"

McEnany paused, and then said, "Stephen, let me put it this way, I have a feeling that the authorities aren't going to have much luck, but I'm at ease when it comes to justice being served."

Stephen understood. "Okay, Sean. Thanks for everything. We'll talk soon."

"Thanks, Pastor. Your prayers for the Lockes' children would be appreciated."

"Of course, good night."

Hanging up the phone, Grant felt truly tired. In fact, he was drained.

So much death. Dear Lord, are we finished with all of this death? He turned, and looked up at the top floor of the hospital. *Your healing is needed for Jennifer, and yes, for*

Dix, and please keep those poor children protected in your care.

Chapter 73

Death was not finished, however.

It was early Sunday morning when Gino found out that both Geraci and Easton were dead, and Dixon Shaw was still very much alive.

Gino moved quickly to get out of Las Vegas. By late Sunday night, he had driven nearly 11 hours, via an indirect route, to arrive just north of Douglas, Arizona, on the Mexico-U.S. border.

He grabbed a room in a dusty hotel using cash and checking in under an alias. No one in the establishment seemed particularly interested in who he was, where he came from or where he was headed.

Gino came back out of his room and briefly surveyed three vending machines outside the hotel office. He shook his head, walked over to and got in the brown Honda CR-V that he drove down from Las Vegas.

He rode less than five minutes, parked on the street and entered the historic, five-story Hotel Gadsden. Gino seemed to ignore the Italian marble staircase and columns in the lobby, and made his way into the Saddle & Spur Tavern. In a small, horseshoe shaped booth, he ate assorted items off the bar menu, and drank three beers.

While playwright and novelist Thornton Wilde had stayed at the Gadsden for more than two months, Gino would be there for less than two hours.

He paid his tab, walked out of the building, and crossed 11th Street to his small SUV. As Gino was getting into the vehicle, a dark figure wearing a brown hoodie moved around the corner from G Street.

Once he was next to the driver's side door, the man took a gun out from under the sweatshirt and pointed it at Gino.

Gino could do nothing. He said, "Tell Dix it was nothing personal. Just business. He should understand that."

The gunman put two bullets in Gino's chest, and one in the head, and then receded back down G Avenue.

Chapter 74

It was a little less than 12 weeks after he had been shot, saved from death by his son-in-law, and had his hip replaced. Now, Dixon Shaw was back to his normal activities.

On this Sunday afternoon in late July, that meant presiding over the party to celebrate the unleashing of the waters at The River Park and Resort.

With cameras rolling, and staff and guests clapping and cheering, Shaw pulled a large lever, which was the prop to signal those in the control booth to start the water pumps and open the gates. Clear, cool water rushed out of the building into the heat of a July afternoon in Las Vegas, forming a waterfall, then splitting and running into two large channels, funneling down into a massive manmade lake.

Shortly after the waters were moving, Olympic kayakers steered their way down the adventure river course to more cheers.

Standing on one side of Dixon Shaw were the executive directors of his two other casino properties – Lou Hammett and Martina Petty. On the other side was the new executive director of The River, a short, black man who previously had been an assistant business school dean.

Candy Welles was not with Shaw, as she had left him soon after his recovery began. She told Dix, "You don't really love me. I don't think you know what it means to love anyone." Shaw did not seem affected after Candy had moved out.

Shaw's daughter also was not present.

Instead, he was talking into a microphone held by a local television reporter. She had short blond hair, a bright smile, a revealing blue dress, long, slim legs, and spiked heels.

The camera went off, and the reporter handed the microphone to the cameraman.

She said to Dix, "Well, thanks again, Mr. Shaw, for talking with me."

Dix smiled. "It was my pleasure, Ms. Jones. And please, call me Dix."

She returned his smile, and said, "Dix it is. Then you'll have to call me Danielle."

"Danielle, would you be interested in having dinner, perhaps tomorrow night, and I could give you a more personal tour of The River?"

Danielle smiled seductively. "Well, Dix, would this be business or pleasure?"

"Do I have to be honest?"

"Honesty is a must with me, Dix."

"Then, Danielle, it is my hope that our dinner has absolutely nothing to do with business."

"Well, then, Dix, I'd love to have dinner."

As Dixon Shaw and Danielle Jones moved next to each other to get a closer look at the rushing waters of The River Park and Resort, a warm wind stirred desert sand miles to the south, not far off Interstate 15. The shifting sands revealed a cracked skull, with three bullet holes.

Chapter 75

At the same time that Dixon Shaw was moving shoulder to shoulder with Danielle Jones, 2,600 miles away in St. Mary's Lutheran Church, Pastor Zack Charmichael was cradling the small, white-robed James Aiken, Jr. with his left arm.

Charmichael gently poured water from a ceramic shell in his right hand onto the baby's forehead. After doing the action for a third time, he gently wiped James' head dry, and shifted Beatrice Aiken's son so the three-month-old could be comforted.

Charmichael said, "The almighty God and Father of our Lord Jesus Christ, who has given you the new birth of water and of the Spirit and has forgiven you all your sins, strengthen you with His grace to life everlasting."

As Pastor Stephen Grant took over the next part of the baptismal ceremony, James managed to grab Zack's pinky, and he was not letting go.

Charmichael smiled broadly at the baby, and managed a quick glance at Cara Stone, who actually gave her now-fiancé a quick wink. Charmichael blushed, and quickly returned his attention to the baptism.

After the Divine Service was over, Zack and Stephen joined Beatrice, little James, and their family for pictures in the sanctuary.

After a few pictures, Stephen stepped aside as more photos were taken. Jennifer came over to stand next to him. Stephen slipped his arm around his wife's waist. "How are we feeling, Dr. Grant?"

"Good, Pastor Grant."

Stephen and Jennifer watched as Zack and Cara were included in several of the pictures.

Jennifer observed, "The three of them have become quite close since Jay died, haven't they?"

"They have. Zack and Cara not only have helped Beatrice with James, but with her entire family as well. It's been something beneficial to come after Jay's death." He paused. "Did that sound right?"

Jennifer said, "It was a little awkward, but I know what you mean."

He looked down at his wife. "You always do, it seems."

After the photos were done, and everyone else had left the church, Stephen was organizing a few things in his office for the coming days. He worked around Jennifer who had taken over his desk and laptop.

After poking around online for a few minutes, she said, "Come look at this."

Stephen moved next to her. "What is it?"

"Opening ceremonies for The River, just a little while ago."

They watched the video on The River's website.

When it was over, Stephen looked in Jennifer's eyes. "Are you sure you don't regret not running the place?"

She laughed. "Please, we went over this weeks and weeks ago. First, I'm an economist, not a casino executive. Second, you have a calling here that we cannot just walk away from, nor do I want to in any way."

"And regarding that calling, we're a team here."

"I agree. You'd be lost without me."

Stephen smiled, "Yes, yes, I would."

"Third, after everything you told me and the information Sean gave us, I have no idea what to think of my father anymore. Has he changed? And given so many questions and issues, what am I supposed to do with this 40 percent stake in the company?"

Stephen left those questions alone, not that he thought Jen expected an answer, as they had discussed them several times before. "Fair enough." He shut the laptop and sat on the edge of the desk. "So, what's our plan for the rest of the day?"

"I have two ideas. Option one: We go home, take a swim, and relax."

"Sounds appealing. Option two?"

"As you drive home, I'll make a few calls, and see who might be free to join us for that swim, relaxation, and maybe a little barbecue. I could call the usual suspects – Joan, George, Zack, Cara, Tom and Maggie, Ron, and whoever else might pop into our heads. Whoever shows up, shows up."

"I say both."

"Both?"

"I'd love to have everybody over, and then later, we'll kick them out and perhaps have a little alone time in the pool."

"Pastor Grant, are you suggesting that we shut off the pool lights late tonight, and do a little skinny dipping?"

"See, you always know what I mean." Stephen leaned down and kissed her.

Jennifer smiled in that way that enthralled Stephen. She said, "Works for me. I'm in for both. Let's go."

About the Author

This is Ray Keating's fourth novel featuring Stephen Grant. The first was *Warrior Monk: A Pastor Stephen Grant Novel*, followed by *Root of All Evil? A Pastor Stephen Grant Novel* and *An Advent for Religious Liberty: A Pastor Stephen Grant Novel*.

Keating also is a weekly columnist for *Long Island Business News*, a former *Newsday* weekly columnist, an economist, an adjunct college professor, and board member of the American Lutheran Publicity Bureau. His work has appeared in a wide range of additional periodicals, including *The New York Times, The Wall Street Journal, The Washington Post, New York Post,* Los Angeles *Daily News, The Boston Globe, National Review, The Washington Times, Investor's Business Daily,* New York *Daily News, Detroit Free Press, Chicago Tribune, Providence Journal Bulletin,* and *Cincinnati Enquirer.* Keating lives on Long Island with his family.

CPSIA information can be obtained at www.ICGtesting.com
Printed in the USA
LVOW04s0354260814

400820LV00024BA/1904/P